Nina's Salvation
for Joey

STEVEN PREVOSTO

This is a work of fiction. Names, characters, places, and incidents are products of the author's imagination or are used fictitiously and are not to be construed as real. Any resemblance to actual events, locations, organizations, or persons, living or dead, is entirely coincidental.

World Castle Publishing, LLC
Pensacola, Florida
Copyright © Steven Prevosto 2022
Paperback ISBN: 9781958336519
eBook ISBN: 9781958336526
First Edition World Castle Publishing, LLC, August 1, 2022
http://www.worldcastlepublishing.com
Licensing Notes
Cover: Karen Fuller
Editor: Maxine Bringenberg

CHAPTER 1

It was fall in 1974 and very early in the chilly morning hours of a Friday. Everything went wrong for me on a Friday. Why? An empty bottle of Jack Daniels that I brought back from Chicago was overturned on the step facing the bushes. Its whiskey smell hovered over me all night long, still making me puke even though nothing was left inside of me. Was I still trying to get rid of me? I was lying on the wooden porch, curled up in a fetal position, pulling my black leather jacket tightly around me. I don't know why. It wouldn't go any tighter. My black wool hat was down, covering my face. I was sweating and still withdrawing from prescription meds, uppers, and whatever else my friend Zebo had given me to stop my depression. And along with drinking my breakfast, lunch, and dinner these past few months, I knew I was dying a slow death. *But no more!* And a tender, slight smile gently stroked my ego as I collapsed into sleep.

Startled, I jumped up from someone kicking me, with a dog's vicious, threatening growl daring me to react. How ironic. A cop with his German shepherd poking me like a homeless man passed out on the middle of the sidewalk in the city! Suddenly, a young woman's voice yelled at me. "Get off Mrs. Drexler's porch, you drunken junky, or I'll call the police!" I stirred slowly while mumbling inarticulately to make it appear I was attempting to rise. She said, "C'mon, Ariel. You can't help him," as snarling and barking accompanied her down the stairs with tapping paws retreating over the pavement, signaling quiet to resume snuggling up against me.

I pushed my hat above my forehead, and gray black smacked my eye. "I'm blind!" I exclaimed as panic turned me around, where thank God, a sliver of misty blood-orange was peering over the horizon. The silhouettes of Ariel and his master were gliding along the pavement beside the street past the neighbor's house. Who names their dog Ariel? I eased down to the porch, and sleep caressed me.

I felt warmth, and a memory flashed before me of my Grandma Nina Drexler wrapping a large heated bath towel around my shoulders that she had just taken out of the dryer. I was twelve. I think. And over the years of cold weather during the Thanksgiving to Christmas holidays while staying with Grandma, such incredible warmth of love would continue to embrace me as a sheet, a small blanket, or just a bundle of little hugs in towels or wash cloths. And each time, it was followed with loving kisses planted on my cheek. And each time, my tears would rush out from missing my mom's love, and Grandma would just continue to wrap her arms around me in her smothering love.

My parents fought a lot while I was growing up. They especially enjoyed fighting during the holidays. So, they'd bring me over to Grandma's— they always brought me over to Grandma's, my mom's mother. Everybody called her Nina. This was on a Friday, of course, and I would be in her kitchen sitting at her little Formica table, practicing playing the guitar and learning how to channel my loneliness and pain into lyrics and passionate rock music so I wouldn't express it in screaming anger, or with my fists beating a door or a wall until I broke my hand. My music was distilled from my insecurity, pain, and frantic worry that my parents were going to leave me. That I was the reason, Mom, Dad, or both would disappear. My father had a violent temper, and ironically, it was because of me. My father was a very good musician — he could've been great. But he fell in love with my mom, and they had me right away. Dad's career of musical greatness in his dreams was permanently on hold. He taught me everything about the guitar and music. And as I grew being nourished musically by him, I could see *and feel* his jealousy and regret. Spontaneous hugs and kisses weren't given from him. I'd have to initiate them during a guitar lesson by surprising him with a hug around his chest before he got up. Other times, after teaching me a more difficult lesson that I'd learned quickly, he'd rise hastily, as usual, saying indifferently, "Okay," and I'd see a pulse of pride flash in a smile, only to give way to bitterness eating away his love for Mom and me.

Nina was Hungarian and German. Not too tall,

but big boned and strong. She was loving and very religious. Granddad was a cab driver, and over the years, Grandma would work two jobs to help pay the bills. Up until five years ago, Grandma had worked on an assembly line at the Mary Sue candy factory, taking chocolate candy off the line and putting it in boxes. It was located on Canton Avenue in Baltimore City, down the street from St. Agnes Hospital. Each morning, very early, through rain, sleet, or snow, she'd walk one block up Marksworth Street to the corner of Johnny Cake Road to catch the metropolitan bus for a thirty-minute ride to the factory. She was retired now.

A cold breeze rushed by, slapping my face, while a spasm of shaking tackled me. I sneered at the bright, yellow egg yolk of the sun, that was like a spotlight on my final performance of living. On my knees, I grabbed one of the square brick pillars with a fluted wooden column that helped to support the roof over the porch. I pulled myself up to get out of the sun, so vomit wouldn't bake on my leather jacket and pants. My guitar case and two duffel bags of clothes were beside the front door.

Grandma should be awake by now. I just

hoped she'd gotten my telephone message that I was coming to visit with her for a while. A few weeks ago, I had spoken with my mom, and she said Grandma was feeling fine and would love to see me. It had been over two years since I'd seen her, but I'd call her every other week or so. It was just uncanny that she didn't pick up the phone when I called yesterday. I hoped she was all right. She was my second home. Frankly, my most stable and loving home. Here I would get a soberer perspective on a meaningful path of life that I should pursue now that my band had imploded from egos, money problems, and devouring relationships fueled by alcohol and drugs. I was just glad I disciplined myself to send money to Grandma whenever I could to hold for me because I knew myself well enough to know I'd give money to my friends in the band whenever they'd ask for it. Sending money home wasn't an option because, frankly, I didn't trust my parents. Well, I'd trust my mother, but my dad could be pretty manipulative and con it out of her by pleading that she didn't show him how much she loved him and that they needed to go away somewhere. He was always arguing and fighting with her. Dad would leave, my mother would go drop me over at Grandma's (on a Friday), go after him, they'd come back together, come and get me, and we'd go home to be a loving family until the merry-go-round of up and down peace, arguing, fighting, and leaving started all over again.

I opened the outside aluminum door with a large, enclosed, rectangular glass frame and knocked on the heavy wooden door with four long recessed panels painted white. No answer. I knocked harder several times using the faded, brown-brass door knocker. As I waited, I tried to remember if Grandma had hidden a spare house key somewhere. She did! Around back, under the potted plant at the bottom of the stairs. I left my guitar and duffel bags on the porch and grabbed the railing while slowly going down the steps so as not to excite an onslaught of retching my guts out.

The front door then opened, and I heard a cautious but demanding, "Who is it?"

I turned around and said very loud, "Grandma! Grandma, it's me. Joey!"

She opened the outer door, and her forehead and eyes were squeezed together. "Joey?" she asked mistrustfully. Then, "Joey! Joey, honey! How are you? Give me a hug and a kiss."

I came over and gave her what she had asked for ever since I was a child. "Grandma, how are you?"

"I'm feeling okay. Are you sick? You smell like you threw up. Come on in. Put your things down on the floor over there and take those clothes off and take a shower. Get comfortable. Have you had breakfast yet?"

"No, I haven't eaten since seven-thirty last night."

"Well, I'll fix you some eggs, scrapple, and toast while you get cleaned up. Put your things in the spare bedroom and bring your dirty clothes downstairs to the laundry room."

"Thanks, Grandma. I'll bring my leather jacket and pants down because of the smell, but I'll have to take them to the dry cleaners." I went through the living room and down the hallway on the left to the spare bedroom, I knew so very well.

After breakfast, we had coffee and stale chocolate cake. It was fine, though, when I dunked it in my coffee. Grandma loved to bake. Even after Granddad died a few years ago, having had close to thirty strokes in one year, which had to be a medical record — or should be — she wouldn't stop baking. And the stale cake would eventually be thrown out to the birds. Today, I was one of the birds. Anyway, that's another reason she enjoyed having me stay with her — so she could keep on cooking and baking.

"Are you still playing the guitar, Joey? Mom called and said your band broke up. Gee, I was sorry to hear that. I remember how hard you worked to put that band together."

"We had a lousy manager for a while, Grandma. He set us up with a couple of concerts that cancelled on us without notice. Then we had to find jobs while searching for clubs to play at, which meant a lot of driving through Columbus and Indianapolis. In Chicago, we finally had some producers hear us. One said he'd hire us if we had a girl singer. Another one said he liked us and that we had a unique sound. 'But there are so many bands right now with a unique sound. What makes you guys any different?' he asked. I had no idea how to respond to that idiot! And another producer said he'd hire us if we got rid of our keyboard player. Then another one said we sounded great, but he would never return our calls, or he was always out of the office. It was crazy!

Obviously, it was all about who you knew. And we didn't know anybody. Then, we had money problems when the van broke down. We started arguing and getting mad at one another and finally decided to go our own ways. I came back home while Zebo and Denny went out to California, Drake went to New York, and Cory came back here." I didn't want to tell her how alcohol and drugs also came between us to break us apart.

"You're not going to stop playing, are you?" A consoling hand reached over to hold mine. "You can play here in Baltimore. I liked how you played here in my kitchen when you were young. Especially on Friday evenings through Sunday. I'd cook for us, and you'd sing to me if Granddad was driving his cab late that night."

"And if he was, I'd still be practicing until he came home around two or three in the morning. Then he'd let me count all the change he made from tips that night, and he'd give me two dollars for doing it."

"They were good times, weren't they, Joey?"

"They always were, Grandma." I got up to go to the bathroom because my eyes were watering.

CHAPTER 2

Being fall, we started reminiscing on some fond memories of Thanksgiving, which was fast approaching. Grandma and I loved Thanksgiving. My best childhood memories were going to her house for Thanksgiving dinner. Grandma's house became an oven and a sanctuary for the glorious smells giving homage to their respected foods being so deliciously prepared for sacrifice to Thanksgiving. It was the one day where the succulent aromas from the feast chased Granddad's acrid cigar smoke from the living room and dining room to huddle in wisps in the upper corners and crevices of the upstairs ceilings. On this day, I didn't hear Grandma say, "Harry, you know I don't like you smoking your seegars in here!" which she said fervently on the days I came down to visit that weren't a holiday with family visiting.

After watching football in the arena of Grandma's living room, and while the men were just sitting around talking and laughing, and the women were cleaning up after the magnificent repast — washing the dishes, drying them, and putting them away — Granddad would herald the traditional festivity of penny ante poker with a revelry call of pennies rattling and clanking in a large glass jar, for anyone interested in playing to follow him into the dining room. We'd play, and fun would rule. After all, how upset can you be for only losing pennies? Granddad would officiate by making sure no one slowed the game down by studying their hand too long.

Then Grandma would enter in an hour or so and say, "All right, Harry, finish this hand, and we'll set the table for dessert."

"Ah, Nina, just give us ten more minutes," he'd gripe, being annoyed.

"No, Harry, some people have got to go to work tomorrow."

And my mom, with some of my aunts, would set the table with a pretty, white linen tablecloth, while another aunt would bring out the large coffee maker. In the kitchen, adjacent to the dining room, Grandma would poise over the sumptuous cakes and pies on the Formica table. Then intuitively, she'd cut just the right width of slices so everybody could enjoy their favorite dessert.

"Thanksgiving was always fun here, Grandma. You worked so hard for us to enjoy each other. And when everyone was getting ready to leave, Granddad would ask us, 'Did you have enough to eat and drink? Did you have a good time?'"

"It was all about family, Joey. And thanking the Lord for all he gave us," she said with an embracing smile, staring at me. Grandma appeared tired, and I asked her how she was feeling. "Arthritis has really taken hold of my knees since you left, Joey. The pain is gripping them so tight I can barely walk and bend down to do my gardening and cleaning. That's why the house looks such a mess."

I glanced around her kitchen and saw that it needed cleaning badly. My mom complained about how Grandma was such a clean freak and had made her spend so much time scrubbing floors, vacuuming, cleaning the bathrooms, and ironing clothes while growing up that she swore she wouldn't spend that much time in her own house doing it. Unfortunately, it showed, and there were many times I had to shuffle dirty clothes from previous days to wear and use a lot of deodorant because she didn't feel like doing the laundry.

"I'll help you clean your house, Grandma. It's the least I can do while staying here for a while. And Thanksgiving will be here in two weeks. The place has to be cleaned up for everybody coming over."

Sadness dimmed the brightness in her eyes. "Nobody comes over anymore, Joey. Each one of your aunts and uncles is taking turns holding Thanksgiving at their house. This year it's Pat. Marty will come and get me in the morning. And you, Joey. You're welcome as well. Everyone thought it was getting to be too much work for me, what with cleaning and cooking."

I nodded, staring at the table, not wanting it to be that way and understanding it would have to be. But what really bothered me was that I really didn't want to face my relatives for the first time in over two years and tell them the band was a failure, and I had to come back home not knowing what I wanted to do with my life. And also talk about my parents fighting again and going away.

"Are you going to start playing the guitar today, Joey?"

"Maybe later. Right now, I'm going to clean your kitchen."

She objected, but I told her I needed to do something to help her while I stayed there.

"All right. You know, it's going to get cold. Winter's coming. Do you need a scarf or socks, Joey?" That was thoughtful of her.

"I could use a scarf, but I don't want you to buy me one. I'll go shopping—"

"No, I'll knit you a wool scarf. It will be very warm. I have plenty of time, so I won't take 'no' for an answer."

Wow, I never had anyone want to make me anything.

"That would be great, Grandma. Thank you." And it would keep her busy while I cleaned her house, so she wouldn't have to feel she needed to help me.

I took a break from washing and scraping stains off her counter to go outside on the back porch for some fresh air. Comet and Mr. Clean always do their job but inhaling their fumes was making me feel queasy. It was sunny with a slight breeze. Invigorating, yet mild. A perfect autumn day. A cigarette would taste good now, but I was glad I quit smoking. It felt good to enjoy the flavor of food on my tongue again.

I could detect the faint smell of decayed leaves flying through the air as some were fluttering down every once in a while, from Grandma's few trees and the neighbors' trees. The trees surrounding the perimeter of the graveyard behind Grandma's house had grown wider and taller, though there were some gaps here and there where a tree had to be cut down for whatever reason. But autumn's wreath of glorious, colored leaves around the old cemetery always grabbed and held my attention.

In Grandma's backyard, however, several of her big linden trees had rotted away, leaving only tall trunks with wide, black, hollow eyes and deep gouging crevasses circling around and running up and down the length of each tree. Fallen brown branches, many small ones but a few large ones — looking like prehistoric animals standing statuesquely with legs angled outward from the body with a long neck thrust out to attack — littered the ground. Piles of dried, shriveled leaves from last year appeared like long mounds of freshly dug graves waiting for tombstones amidst tall, wavy, yellow-tan grass that overran Grandma's flower gardens, drowning and killing her lovely mums that were blazing stars of various colors throughout the day this time of year.

Suddenly, a sense of overwhelming worthlessness began consuming me. Tears started to well up and streak down my cheeks. I am nothing! I wanted a bottle of bourbon. I'd thrown the remaining anti-depressant pills away before I left Philadelphia. I went down the stairs and trudged through the tall, straw-like grass and mounds of leaves and kept walking. I had to move while inhaling deeply. Self-hatred shook me. I started sweating. Then I bent over, and with my hands on my knees to support me, I threw up. And threw up. Trying to throw up *me* again. Exhausted and crying, I slowly rose and took a napkin out of my pocket, wiped my mouth, dried my tears, and blew my nose. Staring out into the graveyard, I realized there had been so many more graves added to this cemetery since I was a child. The peace was so inviting here, and its call so urgent, so soothing. A roaring rush of cool wind directed my eyes toward the colored leaves shaking in the soaring trees beyond. They were like huge, rainbow colored lollipops. I had to laugh.

Grandma needs me. I need Grandma. I have to wash my puke off the front steps and throw the bottle of Jack away. I can overcome this!

CHAPTER 3

I finished the kitchen, and it looked so much better. A few opened windows allowed the fresh air to enter and circulate around the room to drive out the too citrusy odor laced with a healthy dash of Mr. Clean. I decided to work in one room a day, then caress my guitar, playing some of my songs and reworking the riff, melody, words, or chorus in a few. I also had the urge to play some blues that were playing me.

In the living room, Grandma had fallen asleep in her recliner while beginning to knit me a scarf. I put a small blanket over her so she wouldn't get cold from the open window in the kitchen while I went out front to clean my puke off the stone stairway. I had a mop with a sponge on the end, but it could only be used on the wooden porch. I had to go back into the bathroom and find a bristled scrub brush and a kneeling pad to get down on my knees for the stone steps. After four buckets of Mr. Clean and filthy water, I discovered that the stone was flagstone. The sparkles in the stone glistened while the orange, silver, and red swirling colors flashed in the sunlight. Grandma would be surprised, and I could see her big smile beam like it used to whenever Granddad, me, or my mom cleaned or fixed something around the house for her that she hadn't expected. I emptied my last bucket of Mr. Clean, swimming in black, grimy water, over the side of the front porch facing our neighbor. Something told me I probably shouldn't have done it because it wouldn't be good for the grass. But I did, and I couldn't take it back.

I was going to see if Grandma was awake when I heard, "Joey Maks!" A pretty girl, who looked familiar but whose name I had forgotten, was standing before me. "Was that you, drunk and sleeping in your own puke this morning on this porch?"

"It was not as it appeared. Yes, I had been

drinking, but I emptied the bottle so I wouldn't drink anymore. And smelling the alcohol all night made me sick. Also, I am not a junky."

She carried a pretty cloth bag with her that had nice leather handles. "Well, Cory's back. I saw him in Fells Point. He said you, Drake, Denny, and Zebo were partying as if there was no tomorrow. Alcohol, prescription meds, cocaine, and pot. And that you were high all the time. Would even forget what song you were playing during a gig."

"That's a lie! Yeah, I was taking drugs. But never before a show. And things weren't going well. We couldn't get a gig. We were arguing—money problems. Denny and Zebo wanted us to go to LA. So, I came home."

"Smart decision. So, what're you going to do with your life?"

"I'm...I want to try and play a few nights during the week or weekend in some of the bars in Fells Point. Or around here. Then check out some jobs available during the day."

"Good luck. Oh, better make sure you have gas in your car. The gas shortage is causing long lines at the pumps."

"Thanks for telling me. I didn't know that."

"It's on the news every day. Is your grandmother here? I'd like to check her blood pressure and heart."

"Are you a nurse?"

"I am. I graduated from the University of Maryland this year. Mrs. Drexler had helped my mom out while we were growing up, and I told her one day that I would take care of her. So now I come over once a week or so to check on her."

"Thank you. What did my grandmother do for your family?"

"My father had an accident on his construction job, and he was laid up for months. My mom had to hurry up and find work to support all of us. Nina heard about us from church and came over every day with food to fix us breakfast and came back when we came home from school with food to fix us dinner. She was a godsend."

"Yeah. She's really amazing. I'm sorry. I forgot your name."

"Pat Meekins. When we were seniors, you asked me to go to a dance at Gwynn Oak Park, but you stood me up. I got over it," beamed a self-righteous smug. "Could you let your grandmother know I'm here, please? I called her yesterday to let her know I'd be over today, but sometimes she forgets."

"Sure. C'mon in."

She followed me as I remembered that dance. Zebo had met a girl the previous week at one of our gigs. He was crazy about her. I had to chuckle because there wasn't a gig we ever played that he wasn't *crazy* over a girl! He asked her to this dance, but she wouldn't go unless he got her friend a date as well. So, I did him a favor. The girl was pretty and very quiet. And I was very thankful because the headliner band's lead guitarist riveted my attention to how he played the blues with such soul and passion.

Grandma was still sleeping while snoring gently in her recliner in the living room.

"I'll go in the kitchen and check to make sure she's been taking her medication," Pat said, speaking barely above a whisper. As I followed her into the kitchen, she paused and said, "Wow. This is really clean. And smells nice. Did you do this?"

"Yes." A chilly breeze was hurrying through the open window, so I closed it. Pat opened a cabinet to the right of the stove and above it. She took out a small rectangular prescription box that planned Grandma's medication for the week. "She hasn't taken today's, Thursday's, or Wednesday's medication. How long are you staying here?"

"Till at least the end of the year. Show me what she's supposed to take, and I'll make sure she takes it."

"Just these three pills once a day. This white pill is for her heart. She has a heart murmur and a slight hole in one of the valves of her heart. Nothing serious, but she should take this medication and watch her diet. If you can get her to walk a lot, that will help her as well. This orange pill is for her cholesterol—that she takes before she goes to bed, and this pink pill is for her arthritis, which she can take with the white pill. She doesn't seem to need any more medication at the moment. She has my number, and I've written down her doctor's name and number on paper and put it beside her medication in the cabinet."

"Thank you, Pat. I'll take care of her."

"Wonderful. I'll call your grandmother and stop by one day next week. Good luck finding a gig."

"Thank you."

As Pat was leaving, I stared after her. I was happy for her but a little jealous that she had a job doing what she liked. *That's what I need. I probably should look into going to college. But all I know is music.*

That evening after dinner, I persuaded Grandma to walk up and down the block with me. She needed to get out and walk. Strolling up the street, she'd point and reminisce about going to one house for barbecues during the summer, an anniversary party at another, or Harry playing poker twice a month at two other houses.

"We had good times at our neighbors', Joey. We were all hardworking people." Joey realized that he had never heard her say anything mean about anyone. "Now, everybody's gone. If they didn't die or move away, then they went into a nursing home. I don't want that, Joey. I'll live and die in my own house."

"I hope that doesn't happen for a very long time, Grandma."

She started laughing. "I hope so too, Joey."

We walked on quietly, and the stars were calling me. My eyes shot up into their sparkling wonder. What does it feel like to be at peace with what you love to do and have your joy shine through you?

When we returned home, we took showers, and after Grandma went to bed, I worked on a sad melody to some lyrics to soothe my depression over the dismal state of my life.

CHAPTER 4

The next day, Saturday, I rose early with Grandma, around six-thirty. I made us breakfast and then went to the gas station, taking my guitar in case the lines were long. Getting there early was the key to avoiding the long line that was already forming behind me. Luckily, my place was fourth, and I only had about a ten-minute wait. Afterwards, I went to the bank and sat in the car, waiting for it to open. Over the years, I had sent Grandma six hundred dollars. I knew that was not going to last me long, but at least the cash was available for me in case of an emergency. Staring out the window, cars were driving people down the highway going somewhere with a purpose, while I was going nowhere. Then, like a tender embrace, the sad melody that I was working on last night began playing in my head. It whispered that it needed a more passionate punch to rouse more attention to it. I took a pen and some paper out of my pants pocket, which I always carried for when I felt the urge to write lyrics to a melody I heard in my head and started playing and rewriting the song.

When I returned to Grandma's, she was in the kitchen chopping vegetables on the table and putting them in a large soup pot.

"Thank you, Joey, for putting gas in my tank. I'm going to visit two of my little old lady friends this afternoon. I want to make one a cake because it's her birthday, and the other a pot of soup since her hands are arthritic, and she can't cook much. I already cooked the chicken yesterday, so now I'm just putting the chopped vegetables into the pot and letting them all boil together. I think they'll enjoy the surprise. But if you don't mind, Joey, could you go to the store and pick me up a few more things? I'll give you some money."

"Of course, Grandma." I had to chuckle at her "little old lady friends." Grandma had to be in her seventies herself. "I'll clean the living room while you're out, and then I'll bring down the Thanksgiving decorations from the attic. Will that be okay?"

"Oh, that will be lovely, Joey." She scraped sliced carrots into the pot, set the cutting board on the counter beside the stove, and turned to me. "Those decorations haven't been down here in years. I miss them. Harry use to bring them down, and I'd do the decorating. Then when I'd finish, we'd eat dinner and, afterwards, sit in the living room and reminisce over some past Thanksgivings. Harry would sit in his favorite chair and smoke his seegar and drink his beer while I'd had my coffee with a little Irish whiskey in it." She smiled, gazing out the window as the sunlight suddenly receded behind a cloud, and shadow crept into the kitchen. Abruptly, her look became wistful. "Time is so precious, Joey. Take her hand but don't let her hurry. Make her walk slowly. Enjoy and cherish every moment." She smiled as her eyes watered, and she came over to embrace me. "Promise me?"

"I will, Grandma." I didn't quite understand what she meant, but I thought she missed Granddad and didn't like being alone.

She left and returned shortly, giving me some money and a short grocery list. "There's a little extra to buy something sweet for yourself."

"Thank you, Grandma," I said, chuckling, and left.

Inside the A&P food store, I checked out the cost of renting a rug cleaner and rented one for the day. Grandma's cream-colored rugs in the living room and dining room had some brown-tan colored stains or mold that had nestled in comfortably over the years and were spewing out sour smells. Afterwards, I decided to stop by Louie's Bookstore, Café, and Bar to see if they'd hire me to play guitar and sing a few nights. The manager wasn't there, so I left a cassette tape of songs, two covers and six originals, along with my name and phone number. I also wrote that I was a graduate of Catonsville High School. If he knew I was local, he might believe I would have a following and be good for business. I hoped so, anyway. Frankly, I hadn't kept in touch with anyone from school. I was pretty much a nerd who kept to myself and played my music, and studied just enough to pass. I had to. My father barely graduated from high school and would take my guitar away or beat me if I didn't keep at least a C average. It was my fellow band members who were cocky and arrogant in school, the neighborhood, and outside of it that gave the band, and by association, me, the "bad boy" attitude that tattooed us before we left to tour in the Midwest.

While Grandma was baking and cooking, I decided to practice and work on a few melodies while writing lyrics for two rock songs playing in my head. I wasn't even paying much attention when Grandma knocked on my door and said she was leaving and would be back in a few hours. She was gone the whole afternoon. Luckily, it was very mild outside for November. I opened the windows, steam cleaned the rugs, and surprisingly, there was an attachment that allowed me to scrub off the grime and light stains on the upholstered chairs and sofas, inviting a pleasant smell to return and become cozy.

I had just finished cleaning the floors with my new friend Mr. Clean when Grandma walked in with a big smile on her face and gazed around the rooms. "Joey, what did you do?"

I grinned and said, "I told you I'd clean these two rooms for you while you were gone."

"It looks so wonderful and fresh. Almost brand new," she said delightedly, coming over to give me a hug.

I took her into the kitchen while the two rooms dried out. Once we sat down at the Formica table, her face began to beam with joy.

"Joey, I changed my mind at the last minute and convinced Jeannine to come with me and surprise Lorene for her birthday. She'd never met her, but now she has a new friend and somebody to call and talk to. We spent the afternoon reminiscing about the old days. We had such a fun time," she said with a fond smile.

The rugs and furniture were still a little damp, so Grandma said she was going to read a little in her bedroom. A chill grabbed hold of me, so I closed the windows again and told her I was going to take the rug cleaning machine back to A&P.

As I was leaving, the phone rang. It was Louie's Bookstore, Café, and Bar. "Yeah, this is Joey."

"This is Marty Spears, the owner. I like your music, Joey, but after hearing things about you and your band buddies using drugs and havin' an attitude with people while on stage, I can't have that in my café."

"Mr. Spears, wait…please. I use to take drugs, but not anymore. And I never had an attitude toward my audience. That was the other members in my previous band. They were the jerks and goof-offs. Not me. My only goal is to—"

"Listen, Joey, I don't want the people you know and who follow you bringing their garbage into my café. Goodbye."

Stunned, I hung up the phone. *Does that mean the other bars won't hire me, either?*

On my way to the A&P, I decided to drop off a cassette tape and a brief bio of myself to two more of the area's popular bars. Inside Turkey Joe's Saloon, Joe, the owner, said he was booked solid for the next two months.

"Well, can I leave you my bio and a tape of my music?"

"I'm booked," he said rudely and left.

Next, I went to The Vinyl Pub on the corner down the street and asked the bartender if I could speak to the owner.

"What's it in reference to?"

"I'm a singer, and I'd like him to listen to my

tape and hopefully hire me."

"Nobody's going to hire you, Joey," he said with a surly grin. "I graduated in your class. You guys were jerks and scumbags. Cory's back and has already spread the word you and your band buddies were druggies. You couldn't even play the guitar some nights, and that's why you all split up," he said tauntingly.

I could feel my fist tightening to hit him, but what would that accomplish? Cory was who I wanted to punch in the face.

"Do you know where Cory is now?" I asked with a tense stare and rigid face.

"He said he was going to audition for a band in New York."

I left. I wanted to go to Fells Point and play on the streets outside of the local bars, but Cory probably had been there as well. He had friends in bands playing in the bars and taverns down there and knew the bartenders. But I needed the money. If worst came to worst, I'd have to play in the little park bordered with parking places in the center of Fells Point. I went back to my grandmother's.

CHAPTER 5

I was angry and upset and just wanted to play my guitar all night. But I brought down the Thanksgiving decorations while Grandma cooked dinner. I wanted to have fun with the memories of all the decorations, but I was feeling too depressed. It seemed fate was against me, and I was growing anxious with how I was going to make some money. After dinner, I removed the decorations from the boxes and handed them to Grandma quietly. She'd hold each of them dearly while cherishing a memory, then smile and look for a place where people would be sure to see it.

"Joey, what's wrong? You're so quiet."

"The owner of some bars where I wanted to

play my music said they were booked and didn't have any nights available when I could play."

"Ah, Joey, that's a shame. If your grandfather was alive, he'd tell you there are plenty of bars in the area," she said with a smile that had a slight tweak of sarcasm. "Keep trying."

"I will, Grandma," I said, without much enthusiasm.

"Joey, you play very well. Your father plays guitar and says you play better than him when he was your age. Don't give up, honey, please? You've got talent. You'll play somewhere soon."

"I hope so, Grandma." I loved her for that. I only regretted that I lied to her.

We sat around admiring the unique old Thanksgiving decorations, along with a few Christmas ones that said, "Don't forget, I'm coming soon." Grandma then shared a few stories from past Thanksgivings about Granddad and my mother. They were dear memories that made me chuckle, but…. Thanksgiving suddenly didn't mean anything to me. My parents were fighting and not around. I hadn't seen my relatives for more than two years. Music was my only friend. What did I have to be thankful for? My future appeared desperate. I had to make money!

Grandma went to bed around nine o'clock. I sat at the Formica table in the kitchen, playing the song that I rewrote in the car this morning. The driving passion of the music I wanted for the sad lyrics was there. Now I had to break up the monotony of it. I interwove slower music to stress the sadness in other parts, then finally, I felt like it all came together. Such a cool, tingling feeling of accomplishment surged through me! A much more thrilling sensation than to have been satisfied with hitting Cory.

At intervals, a man's voice reciting something in a monotone would barge into the kitchen, distracting me. Finally, I went to see where it was coming from, and it was in Grandma's bedroom. She was listening to the rosary on the radio. I remembered as a child, Mom, Dad, and I would come over on a Friday. They'd drop me off and come back on Sunday to celebrate either Grandma, Granddad, Mom, or her sister or brother's birthday. I would stay the weekend. Granddad would be working very late on Friday and Saturday nights, and Grandma would be sewing and mending Granddad's shirts, socks, or pants, or her own blouses and dresses while I was watching T.V. During the commercials, I'd dart into the kitchen for something to drink or to grab one of her delicious homemade chocolate chip cookies, and I'd see Grandma moving her lips in unison to the sharp, resonating voice saying the rosary on the radio. In fact, it wasn't too long ago that her mother, Mary Drexler, was leaving St. Benedict's Catholic Church going down the cement steps, and at the bottom, on the pavement, suddenly knelt down facing the church, and while saying the rosary fell over dead! She had a heart attack.

Sunday morning, Grandma asked me to drive her to church. "My arthritis is acting up terribly in my knees this morning, Joey. I don't think I'll be able to drive."

"The last time I went to church, Grandma, was with you when I was in high school."

"That's all right, Joey," she said with a smile. "God doesn't hold grudges. He'll love to see you."

I had to chuckle. She was always so positive and had a smile. Just like my mother, even though my father had tried to take it away ever since they'd been married.

Grandma had always gone to St. Benedict's on Wilkens Avenue in Baltimore City, but over the years, the drive had grown to be too much for her. "There are too many people out there on the road, Joey. And some of them are crazy!" she said with an intense stare. So, she'd been going to St. Agnes on Route Forty, which was only about five minutes from her house.

The priest saying nine o'clock mass that morning was Father Love. He looked to be in his late twenties. Right before the gospel, he announced that the choir director was seeking a guitar player for the folk mass on Sunday mornings at ten o'clock. "There will be a stipend after each performance," he said. "For further information, please, read the church bulletin."

Well, it is a weekly gig for an hour. Maybe I'll check it out, I thought.

Father Love's gospel was short. "Christ is love, and he loves you very much. So, what are we to do in return? Pray. Prayer brings us closer to God. Pray for ourselves and others. And if we are to be a disciple of Christ, one who would by example love others as yourself, then with Thanksgiving fast approaching, now is the time to show our love toward others by helping those in need. The second collection of today's mass and next weeks will be used to buy food for the poor in our parish and to help them have heat for the winter."

He made me worry about Grandma. She was just getting by with her little pension and her social security check. I had to be ready to help her pay for heating oil this winter.

CHAPTER 6

Early Monday evening, I showed up at 715 Lafayette Avenue, across from Westview Mall Shopping Center, about six minutes from Grandma's house. A very cute girl with blonde hair falling behind her shoulders answered the door. "Hello. You're Joey Maks," she said sprightly with a smile.

"Yes, and you're Chris Mullens," I said, smiling as well.

"Please, come in." Drums and a bass guitar jamming in the basement had the floor and walls vibrating. "That's my band playing. My two sisters and I are in it."

"What's your band's name?"

"We call ourselves Pebbles."

"No way! That's Fred Flintstone's daughter's name! That was one of my favorite T.V. shows growing up."

"Yes, that's her."

I followed her into the living room. "How long has your band been playing together?" I asked curiously.

"Well, my sisters and I have been playing together since middle school. Then, a little over a year ago, our friend, Denise, joined our band to play lead guitar, and we started learning and playing covers. But we also have some original songs we're working on. We've mostly been playing at parties, Bull Roasts, CYOs, and high school dances. But a band cancelled at the last-minute playing at The Patapsco Inn in the Route 40 Shopping Center last month, and the owner, who knew friends of ours, called and asked if we wanted to play. And we jumped at the chance. They're only a couple of minutes from here. But then, out of the blue, a guy who heard us play at The Patapsco is opening a new club called The Palace and wants us to play *there* right before Thanksgiving! And it's in the same shopping center. How lucky is that! I think we're good, and being the only female band in the area helps. But to be honest, wearing sexy caveman costumes sells tickets."

"You mean sexy like Raquel Welch in One Million B.C.?"

"Not *that* revealing. But close enough," said an alluring smile with a wicked flash in her eyes. "The owner is giving us two shows, thirty minutes each while opening for two popular bands in the area. Come up and see us if you can."

"Wow! That's great. I will." *Hopefully, good looks will perform good music*, darted across my mind. I never heard of any popular female bands performing in the area, or even while I was traveling in the Midwest.

Chris was sitting at an upright piano beside my upholstered chair as I was taking my guitar out of its case. She handed me some copies of sheet music. "These are the songs we'll play on Sunday. They're simple. Father Love says you've been playing so long you'll learn them quickly." She started playing the opening song that followed Father entering the church. What Chris played on the piano, I just accompanied her on guitar or had a short solo in a higher key. Simple. After twenty minutes, I had four of the five songs down.

"Would you like anything to drink?" she asked.

"No, thank you. Let's finish working on the last song."

"Well, my sisters want to rehearse *now* because they *have* to go out this evening," she said, rolling her eyes, apparently upset. "So can you come over at the same time on Wednesday night, and we'll finish it?"

"Sure. That'll be fine."

"Thank you, Joey. Father Love said you were in a band for several years."

"I was. We graduated from Catonsville High School together five years ago. We all were working odd jobs and struggled finding gigs playing where whoever would hire us: fire halls, local Parks, rec centers, and Ocean City. Then two years ago we decided to go for it. Travel out West and play in clubs in cities on our way out there, hoping to sign with a record label. We didn't. Our van broke down, we began arguing over bills, and a couple of guys wanted to move to California. But honestly, we couldn't stand one another anymore. So, I came back home."

"Good. Wherever you're not happy, don't stay. My sisters and I—oh, we're triplets, by the way—we graduated from Archbishop Keough High School four years ago. What was the name of your band?"

"Schroeder Hits the Limelight."

"Oh, okay! I remember you guys. About three years ago, you played at the Baltimore Civic Center in the battle of the bands one weekend. In fact, you won."

"Yes, we did."

"The audience really loved your music. So did my sisters and I. But some of our friends who heard you play at other places said your band members were pretty obnoxious and conceited on stage and off around town."

"Yes, *they* were. But not me. And the songs you liked, I wrote the music."

An impressive gaze and smile bolted across her face.

CHAPTER 7

I came back to Grandma's around eight o'clock. She was reading in her favorite recliner in the living room. "How did it go, Joey?"

"The music is simple. There will be three of us. Me, Chris, who will play the organ and sing, and another girl who'll play the tambourine and sing. We'll practice again Wednesday night."

"I can't wait to hear you all."

"There'll be a little money from it, Grandma. But I'll need it for gas."

"And you'll be at church each week."

I smiled. "Yes, I will. And you'll come with me."

"I certainly will. What did you think of this

girl, Chris?"

"She's cute. Nice. Plays the piano really well. She's a year younger than me. She and her sisters are in a band. They're going to play at a new club called The Palace on Tuesday next week, right before Thanksgiving. It's in the Route Forty Shopping Center about five minutes from here."

"Is that so? Boy, Joey, the area sure is changing around here," she said and chuckled. "Soon, I won't even know my way around."

I realized that was true. I'd noticed so many changes myself after being away for over two years. "You're right, Grandma. Since I've come back, I've seen more housing developments, more shopping centers, and more car mechanic shops along Route Forty. It's looking like a long, overcrowded strip mall."

"And that's more people and more traffic," she said, perturbed.

As she resumed her reading, I went to my room to rehearse some songs. I was determined to go to Fells Point tomorrow, Tuesday, and humbly expose myself to abuse from those who would surely recognize me, thanks to Zebo, Denny, Drake, *and*

Cory, who used the band's popularity down there to ridicule and insult people at will and steal many a guy's girlfriend. But regardless of what fate flung at me, I was resolved to make some money.

CHAPTER 8

It was shortly before three-thirty when I arrived in the rectangular brick and cement park located in the center of Fells Point. It was bordered on all four sides with parked cars. The square rest area and garden were designed with large cement urns holding small trees and rectangular spaces lined with small boxwoods that enclosed various beds of flowering plants during the spring and summer. Wooden benches with cast iron frames were placed comfortably around the perimeter facing toward the gardens. The park conveniently faced each street that was lined with restaurants and bars, so at night when patrons flowed from each, their eyes settled on the lighted gardens. Usually, during this time of day,

I never saw policemen patrolling the streets.

I claimed my space beneath a streetlamp. Its base was beside a bench where I could clandestinely unscrew a plate to gain access to a wire outlet to plug in my small but powerful 1960 Silvertone Combo amplifier that had been my dad's. I moved it several feet to the left, in front of the bench, with my opened guitar case beside it to hide the electrical cord and give the appearance that the amp was battery operated. I'd never played in Baltimore on the street. My father said he did it a few times when he was younger and hard-up for cash.

I brought out my Gibson ES-335, courtesy of my father, and thought I'd begin by getting people's attention by playing some famous songs with familiar riffs and melodies: Chuck Berry, Duane Allman, Led Zeppelin, The Kinks, Rolling Stones, Beatles, and The Ventures. It wasn't long before some street stragglers and drifters in all manner of dress, hair length, cleanliness, and temperament were meandering over, listening, staring at me curiously while nodding their head to the rhythm, then flinging a spoken word or phrase to the stranger beside them, smiling. Some change was clinging in the guitar case, but at this rate, it was going to be a long afternoon and early evening being short changed out of the real money if I didn't get any better clientele.

It was a mild day in the fifties, and soon people from the taverns were strolling out, drawn to the music in the park. Hopefully, they were bringing some cash to lay over the change. An hour flew by, and yes!—the green bills were finally coating the dark silver and worn copper coins. I was smiling and playing whatever anyone in the crowd wanted to hear. It was great. Then, after a few songs, suddenly, something soft and spongy hit me on my back. I swung around, wondering what was going on, and saw snickering and giggling teens flinging pieces of hamburger and hotdog buns with mustard and ketchup pecking and bouncing off my shoulder, then my chest, face, and head. I did see some guys bent over with their backs toward me, fleeing through the crowd, but I couldn't identify them.

"You guys are so uncool! Just chill!" yelled a long gray-haired hippy after those who were throwing the food portions at me.

"Why don't you freaks just let the man play?" shouted a girl with short hair and glasses.

Suddenly, cold liquid splashing on my back, neck, and head shocked me, and I stopped playing, spun around, and saw some guy running while people behind me were shouting, "Watch out!" "Stop him!"

I turned to see a guy grabbing money from my guitar case and running away. I didn't dare go after him. Someone might steal my guitar and amp next. Again, a piece of bread, soft and gooey with mustard and cherry tomatoes, hit me on the chest, and several guys shouted, "Joey burn out, go home! Where's your band, druggy? Get lost, Joey!"

I gathered my money together, put my guitar away, unplugged my amp, wiped the mustard and ketchup off my shirt and face, and left amidst hurling comments begging me not to leave and apologizing for those "punks" who said what they did. But I was embarrassed, angry, smelling and looking like a hot dog with mustard and tomatoes, and I couldn't concentrate on playing while being fearful of what would be thrown next and maybe damaging my guitar or amp.

On the way home, I was so frustrated and angry that I just started crying. I wouldn't be able to go anywhere in the city doing what I enjoyed and make money doing it. Then I burst out laughing. The only place where I could play in public without any abuse was in church. It was my modern-day sanctuary.

Grandma was upset when I told her what had happened. "The nerve of those boys, Joey. Where's the police when you need them? They'll get their just desserts. I guarantee you. Meanwhile, put those clothes in the laundry room, take a shower, and I'll make us a fine dinner," she said with a smile, giving me a kiss and a hug. "And say a prayer, Joey, please."

I had to chuckle to myself in spite of feeling anxious and tense. When I was young, Grandma always wanted to fix me something to eat to take my mind off my loneliness and anger when my parents weren't around. I loved her for it. But now, at twenty-two, I was leaving the table worried about finding a job to support myself. I only made forty-eight dollars and some change today. But the smiles, joy, and clapping from those people watching and hearing me play had made me feel so good. The reality of that not happening again punched me hard in the psyche, and I went to my bedroom and sat on my bed and cried.

Shortly, Grandma knocked on my door and asked me to take a walk with her. Reluctantly, I did. We walked around the block with her telling me how she had to pull Grandad out of his chair at times to walk around the block with her so she wouldn't feel lonely with him in the same room.

"Joey, you see that holly tree across the street?"

"Yes, it's pretty. And big. The berries on it are so red."

"Don't tell anyone, but for years I'd come out late at night while Harry was sleeping and cut off some of the lower branches on the bottom a few weeks before Christmas to decorate my house," she said, chuckling. I smiled and stared at the twinkling in her eye, thinking that was why she was still so young looking for her age. She was like a kid inside. "Joey, don't worry about giving me any money to stay with me. You're a good worker. You'll find something. Or you'll go to school to find out who you'll be. All right?"

"All right, Grandma," I said, kissing her on the cheek and giving her a big hug. I took her hand, squeezed it, and we started walking while my other hand rose to wipe away the oncoming tears.

Later in the evening, I was in the kitchen leaning against the counter, hugging my guitar and trying to put my depression into a new song—nothing sad. I wanted to feel up. Some rip-roaring, dancing music to jump onto the dance floor driven by crazy-happy lyrics. Shortly, the radio in Grandma's room brought the priest's resonating voice saying the rosary in to greet me. I stopped playing and stared reminiscently into the dimly lit living room.

I gently lay my guitar on the Formica table and slowly followed the priest's voice toward Grandma's room. I had prayed at times when I was a child but rarely had I prayed since then. I just felt like I was the only one who could help myself survive in life and forced myself to work hard to do it.

Across from Grandma's bedroom door, I leaned back against the wall, slowly slid down to the floor, and started praying the rosary along with the priest. I was asking God for his help somehow—someway. I couldn't do it alone anymore.

CHAPTER 9

Wednesday. In eight days, it would be Thanksgiving! I didn't want to go over to my Aunt Pat's to celebrate it. What I wanted to do was surprise Grandma by bringing her "little old lady friends" over to celebrate the day. She had three of them. But I'd have to ask her first since she was expected to go over to Pat's.

Grandma and I were eating breakfast, and I said, "Grandma, would you rather spend Thanksgiving here with your 'little old lady friends' or go over to Pat's?"

While holding her coffee, her mouth dropped open. "Joey, I was just thinking about that! I would love to. Would you mind picking them up?" she asked with wide, gleaming eyes.

"No, of course not."

"Charley, my neighbor, has Thanksgiving at his house. So he'll have some strong men there to help the ladies up the front steps. I'll call him. And I'll call Pat too and let her know. I'll also tell her that if anybody wants to come over here for dessert, they're welcome to. Now I have to start planning the dinner, Joey!" Her sudden enthusiasm and energy animated her, so she couldn't stop smiling. "You'll have to run to the store for me again. Oh, I have to call the ladies and make sure they want to come. I'm sure they will. They were alone and miserable for Thanksgiving last year. What will we have? I have to get some recipes together."

She was so excited she didn't even finish her coffee. She rose, opened a drawer, took out a pencil and scrap of paper, and sat down at the table, talking to herself about what she had to do first, second, third, etc., while I cleaned up our dishes. I went to my bedroom and decided to clean it and then practice the music for Sunday's ten o'clock mass, so I wouldn't have to spend too much time over at Chris's house tonight learning the last song. I wanted to get up early tomorrow and check out the streets in Ellicott City and around Columbia Mall, about twenty minutes away, where most of the pedestrian traffic would walk by me while I was playing. I hadn't been up there in years.

That evening Chris's mother ushered me into her living room and said she would let Chris know I was there. While I was waiting, my eyes rested on Chris's upright piano, and my imagination started playing another rocking melody that could pair up in another song with the one that was dancing in my head last night. It was weird how that happened to me sometimes: riffs, hooks, and melodies would sprout from wherever my eyes perched. And being in desperation mode, I was very appreciative when Terpsichore condescended to play me a catchy measure of a melody as a gift. So much so that I took my guitar out of its case to immediately begin playing it so as to engrain it within my memory.

Shortly, I heard, "Excuse me, Joey." I looked up, and WOW! Three beautiful, blonde haired girls were standing over me, smiling and staring down at me. Chris, who was in the middle, said, "Joey, these are my sisters, Dawn and Stephanie. Dawn plays bass guitar, and Stephanie plays drums. I—we need a favor from you. Our lead guitarist, Denise, she's been sick and was diagnosed with mononucleosis. So, she won't be able to play at The Palace next Tuesday. Would you be able to take her place?" pleaded a scrunched face of desperation.

"They're paying us two hundred dollars apiece!" exclaimed Dawn.

"Two hundred dollars!" I yelled. "I'll do it! Give me a list of your cover songs and the records if you have them. For your original songs, we'll have to—"

"Joey! There's just one requirement," interrupted Chris. "You'll have to dress like a girl."

"What! You mean...?" I stared at them and realized I'd have to wear make-up, shave my legs and chest, have my breasts padded, etc. I shook my head. "I...I can't do that, Chris. I wouldn't—"

"You won't have to sing. You're already a good-looking guy," said Dawn.

"Girl!" interjected Stephanie, and all three began laughing.

"We'll do your make-up, stuff your boobs, and give you a wig," said Dawn.

"We'll paint your nails and get you a costume, but you'll have to shave your legs, arms, and chest," said Stephanie.

"This will be such *great* publicity for us, Joey. Nobody'll recognize you," said Dawn.

"Please, please, please say you'll do it!" yelled Stephanie and Chris in unison.

"It'll only be for this *one* night," implored Chris's sweet smile engagingly.

Two hundred dollars! I thought as I bent over and rubbed my fingers through my hair. That would definitely help pay for Thanksgiving dinner and gas. And maybe even contribute to the cost of heat for the winter. It would take me days on the street to make that kind of money, and that was dependent on what street I could find to play on. Not to mention that I wouldn't be playing in the cold.

I took a deep breath and, raising my head and exhaling, calmly said, "All right."

The girls were so excited they knelt down to hug and kiss me.

"We'll practice the songs for church, then we'll go downstairs and practice the cover songs we'll perform at The Palace," said Chris. "I'm sure you'll be familiar with them."

I cracked a smirky smile, still uncertain how this was all going to work out with me being a girl.

"Joey, it'll be fun, really. After all, we're performers in front of the public. It'll be like you're acting. David Bowie dressed like a girl when he performed his songs touring as Ziggy Stardust," informed Chris smiling enthusiastically.

That's true, I thought. But he never wore a sexy cave girl outfit!

After practicing with Chris for thirty minutes, we went downstairs to rehearse. Her dad had built a cool stage. The back wall and the newly built right and left wall facing the stage were paneled with knotty-pine planks of wood with egg cartons glued to them from the floor to and including the ceiling to keep the sound full and sharp while playing on stage. A Shure Vocal Master PA System was right in front of the stage, along with a TEAC W-1200 Reel-to-Reel recorder to record the music, as well as a cassette tape recorder. At least the girls had everything they needed to *look* professional.

After practicing for a while, I asked Chris, "How many original songs do you have ready to play?"

Stefanie and Dawn tossed an odd, questioning look to one another. "Well, they're kind of in pieces really and still need some work," said Dawn, somewhat embarrassed.

"Are the other two bands at The Palace playing original songs?"

"Hardcore plays a few," Dawn said. "They did have one top ten hit on the radio last year, but—"

"But people go to dance to the covers they play because they sound just like the original artists," said Stephanie. "And Wayside, the other band, plays mostly covers."

"Well, if everyone's only playing covers, then the only thing that makes us unique is being a cute, sexy, all girl band. Wouldn't you want to be respected as musicians and make your audience rock with original songs?" Chris's grin grabbed Joey's eye, remembering the original songs his band played at the Baltimore Civic Center when they were in high school. "You said we're playing two thirty-minute sets. Let's play a few covers in each, then play some original songs that I wrote."

Stephanie and Dawn looked skeptically at each

other. "Have you written any new songs since you played at the Civic Center?" asked Chris.

"That was three years ago. I've written plenty. I have a tape of some of my recent songs in the car. I'll let you listen to them. If you like them, we'll start rehearsing them tomorrow night. If not, we'll just rehearse the covers you play."

They agreed, and I went out to the car and got the cassette tape with some of my most recent and favorite original songs and some covers. Then I went home with a smile that said, "Grandma, Chris wants me to play in her band for one night only! And I'll make two hundred dollars." But I wouldn't say anything about dressing up as a girl!

CHAPTER 10

"See, Joey. God has heard your prayers and is giving you an opportunity," she said excitedly.

"Yes." *Even if it is as a girl*, I thought, chuckling to myself. "And it couldn't have come at a better time. That's money we can use for our Thanksgiving dinner."

"Joey, no. I'll pay for what we'll need for dinner. That's your money. You buy the things you need."

"All right, Grandma." I was still going to help her out anyway. "Has Pat Meekins come over to see you yet?"

"Yes, she came today. Said my heart sounds strong and my blood pressure is good. I told her about my knees losing their fight with the arthritis, and she gave me the number for an orthopedic surgeon."

"Call him tomorrow and make an appointment after Thanksgiving, Grandma."

"I'll do that, Joey."

She got up from her favorite recliner and turned on the T.V. As she sat back down, I grinned at the sparkle in her eye, staring attentively at the show *The Six Million Dollar Man* and its star, Lee Majors, as if expecting him to step out of the T.V. and take her hand while sitting down beside her. I had to chuckle to myself.

I went into the kitchen, where my guitar waited patiently for me on the Formica table, sat down, and started rehearsing Pebbles' cover songs in case they decided not to perform my music. The audiences out west really enjoyed my songs. Especially once Cory, Denny, Drake, and Zebo stopped acting like jerks, making faces at the girls, being comedians, or showing off how well they could play the guitar instead of just playing my songs the way we rehearsed them. That really irritated me. If Chris's band decided to perform my songs, I'd tighten up the hook on one of them, shorten the introduction on another, and tweak a guitar solo on a few. I'd even bring over the new songs I'd written since I'd been at Grandma's. I was a perfectionist. The song could always sound better. That was my Achilles heel in being a songwriter. And why Zebo, Drake, Cory, and Denny were pissed off at me having long rehearsals.

The only song I wasn't going to perform or show anyone was the love song I'd written in Chicago entitled "Not Afraid of Being Close." I wrote it for what I couldn't find in any girl I ever met. The days were moving by so quickly, and we were popular for a short while. We were making some decent money that paid for the alcohol, drugs, and girls. Then I abruptly stepped away from that party scene once I met a very pretty and talented musician named Kay. She was so different from the ordinary girls I'd usually meet out there and back in Baltimore. Kay was more like me.

A scoffing jeer ushered in the torturing memory that naturally occurred on a *Friday* night after a gig at a popular rock club in Chicago named Swanks. We had finished loading the van with our equipment, and the guys were going to a bar across the street with the girls, who were wearing mostly flesh instead of clothes, and going gaga over us while we were playing. That night I had this nagging urge to be alone. I didn't want the jarring sounds of shallow, selfish, and meaningless conversation that was always served to me at such a gathering. "I'm going for a walk. Find a nice, quiet place to eat and drink," I said. "I'll take a cab back to the apartment." A few blocks up, I saw a bar and restaurant named Changes with a sign outside that read "Acoustic guitar music tonight." "Great. Peace and quiet." I entered, and there was a small, modest, low keyed group of people inside listening to a guy and a girl playing folk music in the dining room, and only a few people at the bar. I went to the end of the bar toward the back where there were some empty chairs, sat down, and ordered a Dewars and water with a hamburger and salad. Gradually, I was viewing my life as if it were a movie ever since the band and I came out here. I hated what I saw and the person I was becoming. I'd never taken drugs before, but as the weeks went by and the band was getting more gigs, having a following, and getting popular, I felt I should lighten up being a strict manager and join the guys in sharing a few joints, taking some pills, snorting a little coke, having a few drinks, and bonding with them more.

But why!? I was still fighting with them to come to rehearsal on time, telling them to stop goofing off on stage and yelling at them to play my songs the way we rehearsed them.

Suddenly, "Excuse me. My name's Kay. I heard you play tonight. I also heard you play two weeks ago. Honestly, you sounded much better then. You are definitely a more professional and focused musician than the other guys in your band. I just wanted to introduce myself and tell you." Her gentle, soothing stare held me. As she turned to leave, I asked if she would please join me. She did. I asked what she did here in Chicago, and she said she was visiting and staying with friends. She lived in LA, where she played the guitar and sang in a friend's band. We didn't talk long before her friends came up and said they were leaving. She gave me her phone number, and the next day we met at a coffee shop about a block from her apartment and talked for hours, then walked and talked for several more hours. Music played through our conversation. It was our passion! Music and lyrics were one to us. And writing a song was rewriting it, so that special sound or melody embraced or rocked the lyrics.

We talked about the frustration of finding the right musicians you could work with. About guitars and what direction music might be going in the coming year. It was exhilarating. I felt like I was talking to a gorgeous incarnation of myself.

My most cherished memories with her had to be when we'd go to Lincoln Park in midtown Chicago in the early afternoons with our guitars and find a secluded bench on a path surrounded by trees with a lake across from us and write songs. One day while leaving, we decided to sing our songs and others on a street corner close by. We made sixty dollars. Two songs that I wrote I gave to her because she liked them so much. I truly believed I was living what a dream of perfect love was! I began imagining that we were going to live in our own apartment, write music, and just enjoy one another while the band's popularity kept growing, and we'd find an agent who would lead us down the road to fame.

However, fate dictated another course for us. It wasn't long before the gigs started coming slower and further apart. The agents didn't call, and the money was disappearing fast. And on a *Friday*, a warm, sunny afternoon in May, Kay shocked me by saying, "It's been really fun, Joey. But I got to be with somebody who'll take care of me."

"What?!" *Take care of me!* Emotionally devastated, I stared at her, not knowing what to say.

"I'm going back to California. My ex-boyfriend is in a band now, and he wants me to join them. So, goodbye. I'm sorry it didn't work out." She got up from the park bench and left.

In a dazed stupor of walking forever, I returned to my apartment, and in my closet-like bedroom in the dark, I laid down on my thin mattress on the floor and cried. The pillow became so wet I had to get up. I turned on the light and sat at my little table with paper and a pencil on it that I used for a desk. The peeling paint and plaster falling off the wall were like my inner self and psyche stripping away, making me feel like I was nothing. I called my mother, but she wasn't home. Feeling like a walking corpse, numb to any feeling, I went outside to walk the streets. It was very dark when I returned, and Zebo had left me a note saying they all went to a party. He wrote the address if I wanted to join them. No way. With two prescription containers beside the note, he wrote, "If you decide to stay home, here are some uppers or downers to enjoy!" And he drew a little smiley face. Zebo's sudden solution for everything now. I started reaching for the antidepressant, but I stopped. Mom still wasn't home.

My guitar was staring at me from the corner, saying, "I'm always here for you. Just let me show you how much I love you." We sat down at the table, and while all my pain dripped on the paper, I wrote: "Not Afraid of Being Close."

I haven't looked at the song since I left Chicago. I took it out of my notebook and played it. I decided the pain had to accent the more mellow chorus with a brief, hard edge of bass and angry, slashing guitar.

CHAPTER 11

The next morning I got gas to drive Grandma to visit her little old lady friend, Rose Brusini. Grandma had met her through friends at church several months ago. Rose was ninety-one and very energetic for her age, always taking walks. She lived alone and had no friends because, "I don't want any," she said cantankerously. "But your cooking's good, and you're sincere, Nina," she told Grandma. So, Grandma wanted to invite her over for Thanksgiving dinner. She brought Rose some homemade cole slaw and Reuben sandwiches.

I came home after arranging to pick Grandma up when she called that afternoon. Meanwhile, I went into the kitchen and sat at the Formica table with my guitar. I wanted to work the melody that my imagination had played for me at Chris's house last night into a song. As I started getting the intro down and arranging the melody for the verses, I had an epiphany for the hook in the chorus and was writing it down when the phone rang.

"Hi, Joey. This is Chris. My sisters and I like your music. And you were right. When the owner of The Palace hired us, he said, 'I heard you play at The Patapsco Inn, and I want you to play at the opening of my club right before Thanksgiving.' He liked us as musicians but said, 'I'm going to be honest with you. This is a business. The guys coming in here ain't going to be listening to your music. They're gonna go crazy over how sexy you look. *And* they're gonna drink! So, if that don't bother you, you're hired.' Well, we told Dad that we needed the exposure, so we said we'll do it. But with your music, Joey, we could rock that place and have people see us as damn good musicians. Do you have any more songs?"

"I do."

"Can you bring them over tonight around seven, and we'll start rehearsing?"

"That sounds great, Chris. I'll see you then."

"Oh, Joey. When you pull into the driveway, get out, come into the garage, and open the door into the basement. You'll hear us rehearsing."

"Okay."

After I hung up, I anxiously and ecstatically realized we'd have six days to learn fifteen new songs with lyrics. My adrenalin began surging through me. I started shaking. I may never get another chance like this again.

That evening I was driving toward Chris's house, concerned about the band's attitude toward rehearsal. When I arrived, it sounded like they were rehearsing one of my songs. That was a good sign. But once I joined them on stage and started playing with them, I could hear the egos of each instrument vying for attention. The bass was booming and whomping, the drums were pounding, and cymbals were clanging. Everyone was playing so hard, so fast, and so jarring.

Standing in front of them, I waved my arms and yelled, "Stop playing! Stop playing! Please, let me play the song for you first and just listen."

When I finished, I started playing it again and signaled them to join in and accompany me. It was going to be a long evening of playing, stopping, and listening, and playing, stopping, and listening until all the songs were how they sounded in my head. Over two exhausting hours trudged along, but not one of the girls complained. Not one wanted to take a break. They were amazing.

Then, miraculously, Chris, Dawn, and Stephanie surprised me. On the last couple of original songs on the tape I had given them, they were not only listening, but they also injected changes in the rhythm, giving a more driving force that gripped your attention and wouldn't let go. Intuitively, all three of them were putting their own signature on the hook and chorus that was giving those songs some added punch and making them rock way better than Zebo, Denny, Drake, or Cory could ever imagine playing them. Wow! These girls were talented musicians! Now I had great expectations on how they would practice the new songs I brought over.

Abruptly, Chris's mom came up on stage with a taut smile and purpose, escorting it. "All right. It's ten-thirty. Rehearsal's done for tonight." Chris introduced me to her mom, who thanked me for helping her girls with their "first big break" and turned to leave.

"We started off pretty rough, Joey, but it ended up being a *very* productive practice, said Chris, turning off the reel-to-reel music recorder.

"The little changes that you, Stephanie, and Dawn made leading into the hook, chorus, and melody in those last songs were truly inspirational," I said.

"I told you he'd like them, Chris," said Dawn, putting her bass guitar on its stand. "Chris had the inspiration, Joey. She works us harder than Dad. But seriously, learning those songs was worth it."

"Yeah, I was loving it. I hope you didn't mind me going off and doing my take on Keith Moon and John Bonham."

"Stephanie, keep it up," I said to encourage her. "Look over the songs I brought, and I'll see you tomorrow." We said goodbye, and Chris walked me out to my car and thanked me.

"For what? I thank you and your sisters for surprising me with how you made those last songs rock more."

"Well, you had the songs completed. That was the hard part. Whenever we'd try to write a song,

Stephanie and Dawn would always want to change the lyrics or the melody, and we'd never complete the song. That drove my father crazy. He was in the U.S. Marine Band and is *so* disciplined. But he's an officer now and finally got his wish to be transferred to intelligence at Fort Meade. So now he gets home too late to work with us. But he and my uncles are our set-up crew and our bodyguards at our gigs."

"Wonderful. I was worried about guys jumping on stage and molesting me."

Chris laughed. "Don't worry. They're pretty intimidating. You'll be safe. We'll look over the songs tomorrow and start rehearsal at six."

"Sounds good. Your mom didn't look happy when she came downstairs."

"She's happy when we get a gig. But not while we rehearse for it."

"A catch-22." We chuckled.

On the way home, I was impressed with our first rehearsal. Experience, however, burst into my thoughts, warning me that when you rely on others for success, especially in the music business, you will be disappointed. I opened the window and inhaled the cool, fresh night air. I didn't want to think about that.

I was home around eleven. The outside porch light was on, as well as the dim, yellow light from the lamp beside Grandma's reclining chair. She was so thoughtful. The radio in Grandma's room was a little louder than usual. A man with a clear voice was talking about the power of prayer and mentioned three children in Fatima, Portugal, who had seen the Blessed Virgin Mary five times in 1917. The children said the rosary every day, and miracles were witnessed in their village where the sick were being cured.

Grandma had to be asleep, so I opened the door quickly so the long, drawn out screech would only creak and not be louder than the radio and wake her. She was snoring gently as I turned the radio off. I closed the open book lying on her chest with its bookmark and put it on her nightstand. It was cool in the room, and I pulled the blankets over her arms and up beneath her chin. In the hallway, I moved the thermostat up a few degrees to sixty-two. Tomorrow I'd check the oil tank in the basement to see if we needed to fill it for the winter.

I took a shower, thinking I needed to tighten

up the melody on one of the songs I wanted the band to learn. But Chris or Dawn might have a suggestion during practice tomorrow. They certainly proved to me tonight that they could add to the melody and rhythm in a song and have it grab your attention to listen and dance to it. It felt great looking forward to playing before an audience again. And, so far, with a much better band.

In my bedroom, I sat on the bed and noticed a prayer book that Grandma must've put on the nightstand beside my bed. I opened it, and it had a prayer for each day of each month for the year. I turned the pages to November and started saying a prayer for each day since I'd been at Grandma's. Then I said the rosary.

CHAPTER 12

Thursday morning, Grandma said her appointment with the orthopedic surgeon was on the Tuesday after Thanksgiving. I checked the oil tank, and it was less than a quarter full. Grandma called for an oil delivery and said the price of oil was ninety cents a gallon.

"I can't afford that, Joey!" her anxious eyes stressed. "The lady said the oil crisis is causing prices to go sky high."

"We have to fill the tank for the winter, Grandma. I'll have money Tuesday night, so I can help pay that bill."

"No, Joey. I won't let you do that. That's your hard-earned money."

"While I'm living here, I'm going to help with the bills."

With worry wrinkling her face, she turned away, walking slowly to the kitchen window. "I'm worried how high prices are going to affect everything we'll need," she said with concern while staring into the backyard and beyond, into the graveyard. "I'm on a fixed income, Joey. But you can start putting money away for yourself."

I stared at her and only then realized how she always took care of other people but never wanted any help from others. She was always so independent.

"I'll be fine, Grandma," I said with self-assurance.

At least, I hoped so. I didn't know where any money would be coming in after Tuesday night. Chris said Denise, their lead guitarist, would be back in two to three weeks. However, if the audience liked my music, we might get some more gigs before then. But did I really want to be a girl again? The money was definitely too good to pass up.

"I'll go out and clean up the back yard, Grandma," I said to see a smile on her face and take her mind off bills. "I'll rake the leaves and branches and mow the grass."

Turning to me with a beaming grin, she crooned, "Aw, Joey, that would be wonderful. I'm tired of looking at that messy yard. I'll get you some big plastic trash bags. And while you're doing that, I'll polish the silverware for Thanksgiving dinner."

Outside, a brisk wind was blowing with a chill. I wore my faded jeans, a long-sleeved shirt, an old threadbare sweater, and a black wool hat that was pulled down over my ears. That hat had really kept my ears warm while walking the winter streets of Chicago, heading into blasts of freezing air hurled at me by Lake Michigan and the Chicago River. But raking leaves, picking up branches, mowing the front and back lawn, and stuffing the grass and leaves into plastic trash bags was not only making me feel warm but was making me *sweat*. When I was finished, I used the wheelbarrow to haul all the lawn debris and branches to the end of the driveway for the trash men to take away.

"I think the house is ready for Thanksgiving, Joey," Grandma said with an excited smile once we sat down to dinner around four o'clock. "All that needs to be done is the inside and outside has to be painted. But you cleaned all the rooms and helped me put out the Thanksgiving decorations in each one of them. So everyone should feel right at home with a memorable holiday. And it'll all be because of you, Joey."

"Oh, no. I couldn't have decorated the house like you, Grandma. And the cooking? I couldn't cook like you. You're the best. When I was living on my own, I just followed your most simple recipes, like broiling chicken and opening a can of beans. Simple but nutritious. No McDonald's for me."

"Well, I'm glad I taught you something while growing up."

"You did, Grandma. Mom did as well, but Dad would often interrupt her and yell angrily, 'Let him alone, Dolores! He's gotta learn on his own if he's going to be a man!'

"And turn out like him: very indecisive, explosive temper, and unhappy. I don't mean to criticize your father, Joey, but I get angry with how he talks and yells at your mother."

"I do too." I would never tell her how he hit Mom. That would take her smile away and break her heart. "That's why I was always glad to stay with you and Granddad whenever I could."

"And we loved having you. Now, Saturday, Joey, I want you to buy a twenty-five-pound turkey at the A&P. I have a list growing of what we'll need, and I'll give it to you when I'm finished."

"Okay, Grandma. But you have to finish your dinner. It's getting cold."

"Your grandfather would have to tell me the same thing," she said, and chuckled. "I was always thinking of what had to be done whenever the holidays were coming."

"Don't forget, Grandma, we have to take our walk after dinner."

"I know, Joey. Exercise hasn't been my friend these past few years. But I use to move around all the time when I was younger." A wistful smile came to her. "Harry was always telling me to sit down and relax."

CHAPTER 13

Band rehearsal went very well that evening. The girls had practiced all afternoon on the new songs, and Chris surprised me with some catchy additions to the melody to lead into the hook in a couple so they'd rock even more. I was impressed. But ten thirty came around faster than last night. When we stopped rehearsing, Chris surprised me by saying the band couldn't rehearse on the weekend because her mom wanted quiet. The only option we had was to come over to Grandma's house while I played the acoustic guitar and we practiced the lyrics.

"That'll work," Chris said. "Dawn and I can come over around one tomorrow. We'll rehearse until three-thirty. Then we have to waitress at the

Westview Lounge from five until midnight and on Sunday from three until nine. But Dawn and I will rehearse the lyrics together."

"Great. I'll give you two new songs tomorrow to take home and look over. And we'll rehearse on Monday at six, right?" I asked.

"Definitely. But can you come over around five? We want to measure you so my mom can adjust the costume to fit you. We also decided to make you a fur vest to cover up your boobs so they won't fall out."

"I'll just pick them up and stuff them back in if they do." Laughter flashed in Chris's eyes as it tickled her. "Seriously, though, I had a brief panic attack after I woke up from that happening in a dream the other night. I'm really getting very nervous about this."

"Don't worry. Please! Tuesday, you can come over around four. We'll help you dress, put on your make-up, and you can move around the stage while playing to feel comfortable and make sure your costume won't fall off," suggested Chris.

"Whoa. I never thought of that. Great planning ahead."

"We'll remind you to shave your legs, chest,

arms, and under your arms. We'll have a pair of fur boots for you as well. They might be a little big, but hey, we're primitive women, right? So Monday, we'll rehearse late until we get the songs to rock the way we want," said Chris with a gleam in her eye, smiling enthusiastically.

"That sounds great." I loved her and her sisters' work ethic. They practiced hard, made suggestions, or just surprised me.

Saturday morning, Grandma was so excited to hear the girls were coming over that she baked chocolate chip cookies. She sat at the Formica table while I sat and played my acoustic guitar, and Chris and Dawn stood beside me, holding the lyrics to the songs and sang. Grandma smiled, nodded her head at times, and tapped her foot to the rhythm of the music.

"I like them, Joey," she said after we sang a few songs. "If I wasn't so old, I'd get up and dance."

We laughed, and Chris said, "Mrs. Drexler, my father would be glad to come and pick you up and take you home. You could watch our first set. We only play for thirty minutes. You'll be home by nine o'clock."

Chris flung a smile at me as my eyes nearly popped out of my head. *What are you doing?* I thought. I didn't want my grandmother to see me perform for the first time in my life as a girl!

"Well, thank you, Chris. But I have nothing to wear, and I'd be afraid of my hearing aids popping out from that loud music." The girls chuckled as Grandma turned toward me and said, "But I'm very blessed that I can see and hear Joey play and sing right here."

"Thank you, Grandma. But Chris has a cassette player and—"

"Yeah, my dad will bring it. He always brings it to our gigs to record our performance to hear how we can improve on it."

"So, you're going to hear us play, after all, Grandma. And your hearing aids won't pop out."

"Joey, that'll be wonderful," she said excitedly.

Before the girls left, we had thirteen songs memorized. My goal on Monday was to learn two more new songs. That way, I thought we'd leave a lasting impression upon the audience after we left. Hopefully, it would be a good one to get us another gig. If not—back to street searching, where I could play to earn more bread.

Late that night, the phone rang while I was in the kitchen polishing up one of the songs for Monday. I hadn't heard from Mom in a while and hoped it was her.

"Hello?"

It was Chris. "I didn't wake you, did I? We were so busy I couldn't call you earlier."

"That's okay. I was working on one of the songs to rehearse on Monday."

"You are so dedicated, Joey. I just wanted to remind you about being at church a little before ten tomorrow so we can rehearse."

"Sure. Grandma and I will be there."

"Great."

"I bet you're exhausted. You had a long day," I said.

"Yeah. Working weekends, school, homework, and rehearsal — I'm really beat."

"Well, I'll help you sleep so you won't be too tired tomorrow. Think of something good that happened to you today.

"Well, it felt really good that we rehearsed today and memorized the lyrics to the songs. Then

Dawn and I kept singing them at work to remember them, and Stephanie sang them over and over in her head at home."

"That's awesome! Now, did you have a good laugh today?"

"Hmm." A giggle burst through the silence. "When your grandmother said the loud music would make her hearing aids pop out. Then, seeing your boobs falling out on stage."

I started laughing as well. "Okay. You have to hug your favorite stuffed animal while sleeping."

"I do. My raggedy Pooh Bear. Which my mom just finished sewing last week."

"Great. Now, close your eyes and imagine holding a cup."

"What kind of cup?"

"Ahh. Your favorite cup."

"How about a bottle? Because I drink beer out of a bottle."

"That'll work. Now, fill it with wonderful, fun, happy dreams." Suddenly, there was a long, awkward pause. "Chris, you still there?" In the background, I heard what sounded like a stifling sob with sniffling sounds. Crying? "Chris, you okay?"

"Yeah. Sorry. I had to blow my nose. I hope it's not a cold. Uh, happy dreams."

"Yes. You don't have to tell me what they are. Now drink them."

"Okay. What's next?"

"And now you'll sleep soundly and won't be tired."

Chris giggled and asked, "Where did you hear all that from?"

"When I was young, my dad hated his job and took his frustrations out on my mom. They'd argue a lot. If it was at night, sometimes he'd slap her across the face. And she'd scream and run upstairs into my room, shut and lock the door, lay down and cuddle close, then hug and kiss me with her wet cheeks while I was all groggy, not knowing what was happening. Then, while sniffling and drying her tears in my pillow, she'd rub my Snoopy stuffed animal in my face and talk like him, so I wouldn't be scared of Dad, who was suddenly banging on the door yelling that he was sorry. She'd say stuff like, 'Hi, Joey. I'm protecting us.' Then she'd bark like a dog and ask me, 'What made you laugh today? Did you kiss your Snoopy today?' And she'd start kissing me all over while I was giggling. Then as Snoopy, she'd say, 'I had such a wonderful, funny dream with Woodstock.' And she'd tell me the ridiculous things they did. I'd fall asleep, and we'd wake up holding each other, giggling, and feeling happy and safe."

"Oh, that's so sad, Joey," Chris cooed, "but really sweet. What was your dad like the next morning?"

"He'd get up early and have breakfast waiting for Mom and me when we came downstairs. And he'd be crying and apologizing over and over to her while hugging and kissing her, saying he'd never hurt her again. Then he'd hug me and tell me that he loved me very much. Mom's therapy would be not to think about him doing it again. And to keep smiling."

"That's scary, Joey."

"It is. But that's how Mom chose to live, with a smile every day."

"Good for her. Well, I think I can look forward to sleeping soundly now with your help."

"So, I'll see you tomorrow before ten. Have a good night's sleep."

"Thanks. You too. See you tomorrow."

She's a real nice girl. Talented. I'd like to take her out, but she's gotta have a boyfriend. Hell, she has to, being in a rock band and wearing those costumes. Then again, even if she didn't, I didn't have any money or a job—or a car! Three "don'ts," and I was out. I had to laugh in spite of feeling so miserable and wanting to cry. This year and last had been the worst in my life. It couldn't keep getting worse, could it?

I was glad I said the rosary again tonight outside of Grandma's room while listening to it on her radio. She was right. I needed to keep having faith that God would help me if I helped myself and kept praying to Him. God worked in mysterious ways. But how was being a girl going to help me? And that reminded me. I wanted to tell Chris I was wearing sunglasses so nobody in the audience would recognize me.

CHAPTER 14

Sunday morning Grandma and I arrived at St. Agnes Church at ten o'clock. She sat in the middle of the church so she could turn around and look up at the balcony to see me playing. I hadn't performed for an indoor audience in months. I was a little nervous, but Chris was so relaxed I couldn't help but feel the same.

"Are your sisters here?"

"They don't think it's 'cool' to come to church. After all, we're 'rock musicians,'" she said, mock seriously. "And they're wilder than me. They go to bizarre parties with drugs but swear they never take any. Hang out with the cutest and shallowest guys. And that's okay. We're still very close. But Dad's more strict with them than me," she said, smiling. "They have a curfew of midnight except when we have a gig."

The small bell rang, announcing that the priest was present and for everyone to stand as he walked down the center aisle to the altar. Chris began to play the opening hymn on the organ. Someone tapped me on the shoulder. I turned around, and a girl who was a little plump, not too tall, with short brown hair and green eyes, smiled and whispered, "Hi, my name's Cindy. I play the tambourine and sing. I'm sorry I'm late."

"My name's Joey. We just started."

Being my first performance, mass seemed to go by quickly while I was focusing on my cue for when to join in on the next hymn with Chris. I did see Grandma turn around and glance up at me with a smile and wink after I did my first solo during communion. Chris returned from communion and gave me a smile and a nod of approval. Cindy's smile also rapped me on my back, nodding her assent.

After mass, Chris, Grandma, and I were walking toward our cars in the parking lot, and Chris said, "Now, don't forget. You'll be over at four o'clock tomorrow, right?"

"Of course. It's going to be a very memorable experience," I said ironically with a smile, thinking of the time-consuming application of cosmetics necessary for my female transformation.

Chris's hand gently rubbed up and down my back as her soft laugh embraced me, saying, "We're going to make that crowd rock, Joey." She squeezed my hand and walked toward her car.

"Gee, she's a nice girl, Joey. Why don't you ask her out?"

"I don't have the time, Grandma. And she probably has a boyfriend."

"Joey Maks!" she exclaimed, stopping and turning to me as if I had said something that shocked her. "No girl with a boyfriend would let her eyes and smile embrace you with such joy if you were only a friend. She likes you."

"Grandma, she likes my music, and because I can take the place of her sick guitar player," I said, because I was still too emotionally unstable and fragile to hear Chris say that she had a boyfriend or that she didn't want to date guys in her band.

"You are wrong, Joey," Grandma said

enthusiastically. And I bet the two of you a good home cooked dinner that she'll go out with you."

I had to laugh. "All right. I'll ask her out," I said, more to please her than actually intending on asking her out. After Kay had left, taking all of me with her, I literally had nothing to give to another relationship. I liked Chris. She was not only really pretty, smart, and hard working, but I enjoyed her warm, easy going and pleasant personality and conversation. But I got this uneasy vibe from her like she felt it was better to be safe, nice, and polite around me rather than trusting her feelings and being in a relationship with me. Maybe protecting herself from getting hurt. And I, more than anybody, could understand not wanting to experience going through that hell again. Luckily, I couldn't afford to be in a relationship. I needed time.

Monday afternoon at close to four o'clock I arrived at Chris's house feeling very nervous. I had shaved my legs, chest, arms, and armpits that morning. My armpits felt really uncomfortable after I shaved them. Itchy and like sandpaper. I didn't know what to expect, so I was just going to let the girls have their way with me in changing my sex. They were excited to show me the costume their mom, Mary, had sewn for me. The fur bra had Velcro in the back for easy attachment and taking off. She also padded the bra so that my breasts, though not voluptuous, had enough bulge that my lean physique had a cute, effeminate shape. Mary had also made me a fur vest that came down just below my ribs. The girls didn't have vests. Their outfits were sexier than mine, with only the fur bra and fur miniskirt. However, we all wore sheer pantyhose and ankle boots.

Chris and Stephanie then led me over across from the stage to sit at a table that had a large, rectangular mirror with bright light bulbs bordering it. They each sat down on one side of me, and with hands reaching into a cluster of colorful make-up utensils and products blooming on the table around the mirror, they began painting my metamorphosis. After about thirty minutes, Stephanie rose and went over to a clothes tree to carefully bring over my wig of long, blonde hair. She asked me to stand up and placed the wig on my head, adjusting it meticulously to fit snugly. I felt its weight cascading down to the middle of my back.

"There you are, Josephine," teased Stephanie.

"Now go gaga over yourself before the mirror, honey." The girls laughed.

I sat down and couldn't believe it was *me* in the mirror. It was such an uncanny feeling. I was attracted to myself. "You girls have made me extremely pretty."

"Cosmetics are a girl's best friend, honey," quipped Dawn. "It's all about sex appeal."

"I'm afraid to open my mouth without shocking the hell out of people."

"Well, you're not singing, and you won't speak because we're telling people that you have laryngitis," said Chris.

"That'll be a first for me on stage. Not singing," I said, somewhat downcast.

"Cheer up," said Chris, coming over and nonchalantly resting her chin on top of my head, staring at me in the mirror and being silly, sticking her tongue out at me while making funny faces. "Your music will be doing all the singing and talking for you."

Then abruptly, while staring at me, she got really serious as if pricked by a sharp, painful memory and turned away angrily. Whoa! Where did that swift shift in attitude come from? I turned around, and she flung over her shoulder, "C'mon, Joey. We're wasting time! Practice moving and playing on stage to get used to your outfit!" I flung a glance over at Dawn, who was tuning her bass, while a crazy rhythm seemed to take hold of Stephanie as she was pounding it out on the drums. They didn't seem to notice that Chris was upset. I was completely in the dark about what had just happened.

I knew we'd be rehearsing late because of the two new songs and going over the lyrics to some others. Rehearsal was moving smoothly—the girls had really been working on the songs. Of course, being familiar with them, I'd go off on little tangents embellishing the melody in some to see how it would sound. Abruptly Chris stopped and said, "Joey, enough! Please. Stick to how we rehearsed it! That's how we want to play them and not screw up."

With an embarrassed smile, I said, "Sorry," as Dawn and Stefanie's eyes flung an exasperated glance my way.

Then, after a few more songs, we were playing one of my favorites. So naturally, I wanted to enjoy the moment—probably a little too much—by showing off a teeny bit, when bam! Chris stopped playing and came right up to my face, shouting, "Joey! What are you doing?! If you're going to jerk off and do your own thing in your songs, don't do it now! We don't have the time! Just stick to how we've been rehearsing them for the past week. Okay?" And she strode back behind her Hammond B3.

Whoa! I guess I deserved that! "I'm sorry, Dawn. Stephanie."

An irritated, nodding look from Dawn walked around the stage as Stephanie's vexation, stared at her drums. It was ten-fifteen. I suggested we play a different song, but we weren't playing for more than thirty seconds when Chris was off key, Dawn was playing the base line to another song, and the walls were trembling from Stephanie's drums playing to the rhythm of music other than what we were rehearsing. They were done. Spent.

"Okay, time to quit! We're all tired," I said. And being under these hot stage lights didn't aid in cooling down our temperaments either.

"Tired of you playing more than what you're supposed to on the song while we're still learning it!" snapped Chris angrily.

My eyes shot at her. Yes, I was being conceited. But that didn't warrant me being scourged at the pillar of her rage. What was really bothering her?

"Okay. You're right, Chris. I apologize. I shouldn't have done it. It's a bad habit with me sometimes. Will we have time to rehearse the last song before we leave tomorrow?" I dared ask, expecting Chris to throw her Hammond B3 at me.

Stephanie and Dawn tossed tired "Do we have to?" eyes at Chris, who paused and asked calmly, "Were you comfortable moving around with your costume, Joey?"

If I moved very little, I could tolerate the pantyhose pinching my testicles. But for tomorrow night's impromptu, musically spontaneous antics, I better put something soft in there so I'd be comfortable. I lied to Chris and said, "The costume is fine. I'm just worried about looking sexier than you three on stage."

That ignited their laughter, and I thought that was a good way to end the night.

"Can you be here around five o'clock, Joey? We'll rehearse, do your make-up, eat, relax, and then leave," said Chris with a slight smile, a little more at ease.

"Sounds good. I'll see you tomorrow," I said, and started toward the door leading into the garage.

"Ah, Josephine, do you want to take your costume and make-up off before you go, hon?" asked Stephanie while wiping the sweat off her drums, cymbals, and her arms, face, and hair.

Bashful and feeling a little cocky, I said, "Ah…I was going to take her home and see if we could hit it off together." Then I quickly added, "No! Just kidding." The girls laughed. "We're going home together to discuss when's the best time to show off and not to show off in front of your band members."

"Very true, Joey," smirked Dawn, who was wiping down her bass guitar and then putting it in its case.

"Sit at the table, and I'll be right with you," said Stephanie. I sat down, and Dawn shortly came over to join me. She grabbed several Kleenex and plunged them into the jar of Ponds Make-up Remover and began cleaning one side of my face as Stephanie came down, took some tissue and Ponds, and was cleaning the other side. I watched them very carefully.

"That looks easy. I can do it myself next time,"

I said.

"It's always faster coming off," said Stephanie as she carefully took off my wig, returning it to the clothes tree while Dawn was turning off the amps, reel to reel, and the lights on stage.

After I changed and dressed, I said goodbye to Dawn and Stephanie, but I didn't see Chris. She was probably still upset with me.

"Chris must be in the bathroom. I'll tell her you said bye. See you tomorrow, Josephine."

I opened the door to the garage, and it was dark. My car was visible at the end of the driveway behind the lighted black lantern close to the street. As I came out of the garage, I heard a gentle plea behind me.

"May I walk out with you, Joey?" Startled, I turned and saw Chris.

"Chris! Sure."

We walked together slowly, in silence, as a brisk chill greeted and escorted us beneath the glistening stars fanning out across the heavens. At the car, her eyes caressed me.

"I apologize for getting angry at you, Joey. Sometimes I'll say whatever to hurt others because

I hurt. But it has nothing to do with you. It's from choices I made while dating this guy. He's still in my life, but he's not. I want—I need to bring happiness back into my life. That's why I go to church. I pray, talk to God, and ask for His guidance. And you came to join our band, which really brought my sisters and I closer and made us happy. It's like we're finally fulfilling a dream. You're helping us to be just as professional as those two other bands performing tomorrow night. Even better now that we're playing your original songs. Otherwise, we'd be just pretty, sexy, smiling dolls playing cover songs."

"I appreciate you telling me this. The last thing I wanted was to get you and your sisters mad at me. But I deserved you being pissed off at me for showing off on those songs. You guys were busting your ass really hard learning all those songs on such short notice. Plus working at your jobs and going to school, which I should be doing. I'm very happy you gave me this opportunity to be in a band again, to hear people enjoying my music, even if it is only for one night. But the money will really help with bills while living with my grandmother."

"Your grandmother is so sweet and loving,

Joey."

"She is. She only cares about making other people happy. And what's really amazing is after I arrived at my grandmother's, I started praying. Like you. I was saying some of the rosary to ask God to help me so I wouldn't kill myself because I felt like such a failure after my band split up. Then, like a miracle, she asked me to take her to church, and that's how I found you." Suddenly, that inevitable awkward pause stepped in between us, and I couldn't stop myself. "Would you like to go out one-night next week and get something to eat and just talk?"

"I don't think so, Joey. It's not a good time for me right now."

"Okay. Maybe later."

"We'll rehearse tomorrow and do our best at The Palace. We'll enjoy the audience and the moment," Chris said resolutely, with her eyes turning skyward and slowly wandering across the heavens.

"Good idea," I said, making it appear like I was embracing rejection pleasantly. "I'll see you tomorrow."

I opened the car door when suddenly she clutched my arm and said excitedly, "Joey, look!"

And she pointed up at the sky behind me. "The constellations Pisces and Cassiopeia! And a falling star! We have to make a wish." Her eyes began drifting across the universe. "Life's surprises are so precious."

Grandma had said something like that, too, I recalled. My eyes shortly descended, resting upon Chris and embracing her. "Unfortunately, like that star, that's how fast my dreams have been falling for the past year," I said, realizing that I had probably ruined a special, caring moment with her.

"Well, unlike that star, you can raise yourself back up," she quipped, and chuckled. "Goodnight, Joey. I'll see you tomorrow."

I watched her walk toward her house and thought she'd make a guy feel really special in a relationship. Then the thought burst into my mind that the guy she was with might not be making her feel really special in their relationship. Well, that was something that didn't have to concern me now anyway.

I entered Grandma's house feeling very tired. And being nervous and uneasy about tomorrow night's performance didn't help. I—we were in fifth gear during these rehearsals. The girls were memorizing so much music and lyrics for these songs in such a short amount of time, then playing them in front of a *huge* crowd in a *new* club right before Thanksgiving. Talk about pressure! I was already envisioning the girls forgetting the lyrics or substituting other words for them and even playing the wrong song while singing different lyrics. It was going to be a disaster! The fates seemed ready to cut the thread on my career as a musician. Thank God I was wearing a costume to hide my identity.

I plopped down into Grandma's comfortable recliner, along with the prospects of my dismal life and even gloomier future, while my eyes landed on the rug. In the intricate, colorful designs, an eerie, supernatural face suddenly stood out with fangs, black wings growing on the back of its head, and wide, yellow, terrifying eyes. Now, what did that portend? Suddenly, faint, relaxing sounds of a voice saying the rosary came from within Grandma's bedroom. She'd been forgetting to turn her radio off lately and falling asleep. I was about to open her bedroom door, go in, and turn it off when I paused and leaned back against the hallway wall to join in, saying the rosary earnestly to myself. I prayed and pleaded with Jesus to give me faith in Him and to let me honor Him with my talent and to help the girls have confidence in themselves, relax, and do their best.

CHAPTER 15

Chris and her sisters had already been rehearsing for more than an hour when I came over. I jumped in, and we rehearsed the last song of the two I had given them. Chris had a good suggestion for tightening up the melody, and it sounded great. We were ready. But the real test would be on that stage that night.

While Chris and Dawn were helping me with my outfit and make-up, their father and his two brothers were taking microphones and stands, amps, guitars and stands, etc., along with Chris's heavy Hammond B3 Organ, outside and loading them in a van.

The Palace was located in the Route Forty

Shopping Center between Universal Fitness and Val's Pizzeria. Chris's father, Ed, drove us in his 1969 brown Chevy station wagon behind The Palace, and backed in beside the white van that transported our equipment. Its two rear doors were swung open as two tall, muscular men in their mid-forties dressed in army fatigues were already unloading our equipment and carrying it through an open door into The Palace and setting it up for us on stage. A security guard was nonchalantly overseeing what was being brought inside midst the brilliant white light blazing down and behind the building for security and safety.

"It's great how Uncle Joe and Uncle Lou always arrive so early to help you load our equipment and get it to where we play so early, Dad," said Dawn.

"The military teaches you that to do things early and be at places early more often than not helps you avoid problems," declared Ed sagaciously, nodding his affirmation of its truth toward his daughters.

The approaching rumble and roaring of thunder in a Pontiac Judge GTO seemed to vibrate the car as we stepped out. Seeing us, the car stopped and two young men in their early twenties, lean and brawny, jumped out, with one shouting demandingly and raucously as if he'd been drinking.

"Pebbles! Can we have your autograph?" He was holding a pen and paper as both were hurrying toward us with an unsteady step. "I'd be thankful if you could write your phone number down too. I'm Rick Darby."

Chris's father whisked over in front of us. "Some other time, boys. Pebbles has to set up and get ready to open the concert."

"So, let them tell us," said Rick, taking a step forward and planting himself. "Th-the- they can speak for the-themselves," stammered, slurring speech.

"I know they can. But I'm telling you," said Ed as Joe and Lou, two Goliaths, walked down slowly to stand beside Ed to help reinforce what he said, if necessary.

"You guys are lucky I don't have my sling shot," said Rick humorously. "You remember David and Goliath." The girls chuckled.

"Why don't you two go out front and be among the first in line, so you have a good place to watch Pebbles play," said Ed sensibly, wanting to defuse any conflict.

"Pebbles, my name is Frank Solino," said Rick's muscular buddy taking his sturdy arms and thick fingers and proudly piercing his chest, planting his feet to stand-up straight. "And...and we'd be... *elated* to take you girls out on a date anywhere you want to go in my Judge. We'll run into you soon," he said with the hint of an inebriated slur while firing his index finger into them, smiling and slowly backing up unsteadily and falling into the idling and reverberating boom-boom-boom of his thundering car, joining his companion in taking a swig from a bottle. Shortly, they exploded up the not too wide roadway behind the shopping center, squealing and peeling rubber and being obliterated in a wake of smoke.

"Girls, listen to me. *I'm the judge!*" Ed said adamantly with his index finger fixed firmly in his chest. "And if I see or hear of any one of you in that car with those drunken idiots, you'll be grounded for life!"

"Oh, Daddy, we'd much rather steal their car than be with them," Dawn said sarcastically.

"And I won't be 'run into' by them," chuckled Chris as the other girls laughed.

"I swear those drunken fools are going to wreck that beautiful car before this night is over," said Lou angrily. "I'm going to call my buddies at the Baltimore County Police Department and tell'em they'll make a fortune handing out tickets to drunk drivers leaving here tonight."

The security guard, who seemed to be in his thirties, came over and introduced himself. "Hi, I'm Mitch. I've never seen an all-girl rock band before. But if they're all as pretty as you, I hope they keep coming here to play."

"Why, thank you, Mitch. Will you be able to watch us play tonight?" asked Stephanie with her sweet and seductive smile.

"I can sneak away for a little bit," said a bashful grin. "But I have to keep an ear open for the bell on the security door in case of an emergency, or a limo driver, or if a band's manager needs to talk to the band." He ushered us through a dimly lighted hallway and shortly stopped before a white door with a red number three painted on the front at about eye level and opened it for us. Inside was a small but comfortable room with a coffee table in the center with some napkins, paper cups, and a medium size basket woven with thin wooden strips that contained several small, individual bags of Cheez-its, Goldfish, and pretzels. On the wall to the right was a plush black leather sofa. Against the wall adjacent to it were three wooden chairs with thick, black leather cushions on their seats, and against the wall directly across from the door was a small refrigerator. To its left was a make-up table with a mirror and light bulbs bordering it and a bathroom with a small sink and toilet through a door on the left wall.

We sat down and tried to relax. Ed said he would come back and let us know when we'd have a sound check. Feeling antsy, I got up and checked out the refrigerator, asking if anybody would like a Coke, Pepsi, Dr. Pepper, Tab, or Mountain Dew.

"No thanks, Joey," said Chris. "I'm too nervous to eat anything. We've never played before a crowd this large."

"Yeah, it is so far out!" exclaimed Stephanie.

"I just have to get through the first song. Feel the audience's reaction, which I hope will be great, then rock the hell out of them," said Dawn nonchalantly.

"No, *Pebble* the hell out of them," I said, trying to be humorous as Chris and Stephanie started laughing.

"What?" said Dawn, looking at me as if I were totally weird.

"Pebbles—small rocks—our band's name," said Stephanie, enunciating exaggeratingly slow so Dawn would get it while we kept laughing.

"Oh, yeah, yeah, yeah," she guffawed. "Boy, Joey! You've been so serious since we've met that we were wondering if you'd ever lighten up!" Dawn rose to sit at the make-up table and primp.

"I've been beating myself up pretty hard since I came back to Baltimore," I said, looking at each one of them. "And on you guys as well, with setting high expectations during practice. I also should've acted more professionally during rehearsals instead of showing off at times. So...so let's just have fun tonight. If we screw up on the music or lyrics, then we keep playing."

Stephanie and Dawn each threw a kooky glance at Chris.

"Joey, we're not going to screw up! We've worked hard to be here tonight. And with your songs, we're hoping to get more gigs after this show," said Chris proudly.

"I've been thinking about that. Once Denise returns, you girls can keep playing my music, but you'll have to wait until after I get them copyrighted."

Dawn and Stephanie suddenly flung at Chris a quick, questioning gaze. "Joey," said Chris, "The three of us were talking and decided that after tonight if you want to be a part of our band, we're telling Denise that we have a guy who can take her place and play original music that will help us get more gigs in the better clubs in Baltimore."

"And you won't have to dress up as a girl anymore," quipped Dawn sensually.

"Thank you, but let's see how the audience reacts to the music," I said, not too confidently.

"Well, thanks for being excited about our idea," said Chris sardonically.

"No, wait. I think it's a great idea, Chris. I want to. I just— There are people out there who don't like me because of what my old band members did to them. Not me. But I'm afraid once they recognize me in your band, they'll take that out on you guys when we're on stage together."

"Joey, my father and uncles will deal with them. We enjoy your music! And after tonight, other people will too. You just have to trust in yourself and God that if you do your best, you will prevail," said Chris.

"Chris is right, Joey. My dad and uncles will take out anyone who messes with us or disrupts our gigs. Inside or outside of the place," said Stephanie threateningly.

"Joey!" exclaimed Chris after a few moments. "We have to think of a girl's name for you when we introduce you on stage. How about Joan, or Barbara, or—?"

"Call me Donna," I said abruptly, not really caring what name they gave me.

"That name shot out quickly! Why Donna?" asked Stephanie with a curious glint in her eye.

"Donna Provance. She was my first crush in fifth grade."

"Well, Donna Joe," said Dawn teasingly, "now you know how Frank Solino felt when he saw you outside, and will see you tonight, and will follow us and you home, and will—" The girls were laughing.

"No, you said Ed and your uncles were going to protect me!" I protested as fear started pricking me with visions of Frank coming backstage and manhandling me.

"Don't worry, Joey. Frank was drunk when he saw us behind The Palace, and by now, he'll be so plastered he won't even know we've left after our second set," laughed Chris. "And after tonight, when you're out of your costume, he won't ever recognize you again. Besides, we're going to tell anybody who approaches you after our first set that you have laryngitis."

"Great," I said, feeling a little at ease.

"I suppose after your concerts out west, you'll miss the pretty girls rushing back to see you after the show," Dawn said, trying to be nonchalant but with a lustful twinkle in her eyes.

"There were a few," I said, somewhat embarrassed. "They were flighty and mindless. And we paid for them." I turned toward Chris. "But the one girl I am looking forward to seeing when I come backstage tonight is standing right here." I looked at Chris to let her see I'm trying to lighten up and wanted to have fun with her.

Chris gave a subdued smile as she rose from the couch and went to the mirror to check her costume and make-up.

"Ah, now that's really sweet," said Stephanie, with a delighted grin in her bright eyes.

"See, Chris, you got a steady, sincere groupie with heart." Chris ignored Stephanie and turned away from the mirror to sit in a chair, deep in her own thoughts.

I hoped I didn't sound like I was putting pressure on Chris to see me. With the guy she was seeing, I knew that wasn't going to happen in the near future. If at all.

"Well, if you do stay in the band, it's a shame you'll have to be a guy. Because you are a very cute girl, Donna," chuckled Stephanie.

"Oh, speaking of which," said Dawn, "since you're not singing, pick out a guy in the audience every now and then and stare at him, smile, and wink at him. Even point at him. They get excited over that and become our loyal fans."

"Donna is wearing sunglasses, so nobody recognizes her," said Chris matter-of-factly.

"Oh, won't you be the *dark and mysterious one!* The guys will love you. Well, the three of us will do the seductive staring," quipped Dawn.

A long pause abruptly came between us, and

I glanced over at Chris, who was staring at the floor with a sad, wistful look. *Why*? I wandered.

A loud knock on the door startled us, and Ed popped his head inside and said, "You have about twenty minutes on stage right now for a mic check and sound quality check from the PA. So, let's move it."

As the girls were entering the hallway, I was getting a drink of water. Suddenly, whistling came screeching into the room, along with "Hey, pretty ladies! Come my way. Not down the hallway!" exclaimed a demanding, guttural voice.

"In your dreams!" was derisively flung back from what sounded like Dawn's voice.

"I'm dreaming now!" rang with raucous laughter.

The door had been left open a little, and I hid behind it, not wanting to walk out and prompt more lustful gibes. Through a very narrow opening between the door and the doorjamb, I could barely see members of one of the headliner bands walking past.

"They must be Pebbles. That all-girl band," said one of three guys who were dressed in bright colored, sparkling, and glittering clothes with shirts gaping and coiling, black, Brillo pad-like hair bulging out. The lone girl following them had long, straight, jet black hair and a silver glitter Willow bell sleeve dress with silver gleaming knee-high boots.

"I've never seen or heard of one," another guy said gruffly. Have you, Ricky?"

"The only girl band I've ever seen was in a bar on the block. They strutted their sexy asses around the stage holding instruments that they didn't play and I'm sure *couldn't* play, while music was blaring all over the place. And from what I heard about the greedy mafia owner of this place, it'll probably be the same deal here!" said a high, sharp voice.

"Hey, he's a businessman. And he's got the place packed for us! Bring on girl bands! I love 'em!" roared down the hallway.

"Maybe you should form your own girl band, Ricky. Then you'll have your own harem," said the girl mockingly as laughter escorted them into a room. When I heard a door close, I came into the hallway, shut our door, and hurried down the hallway to join the band on stage.

CHAPTER 16

The sound check went well, and we cranked up the volume on the amps. Inside our room backstage, I shared with the girls what one of the guys from the band had said about all girl bands while they were walking to the stage.

Stephanie rose from the couch facing the wall behind which was the room where the other band was staying. She cupped her hands over her mouth and screamed, "You sexist pigs!"

"They're animals!" yelled Dawn disgustedly.

The girls were definitely pumped. Suddenly feeling worried that the audience *wouldn't* take us seriously, Chris suggested taking some of the really rocking songs from our second set and playing them in the first set.

"No. What we have in the first set will definitely make them want to stick around and hear what we'll play in our second set," I said confidently.

While waiting for "time" to knock on our door, we went over the lyrics to a few songs while I practiced a melody to a few of them on my Fender Stratocaster, with Dawn accompanying me by attacking her bass guitar. She definitely came across to me as the cliched "Ditzy blonde," but she could play bass with more passion and command than Zebo ever could in my old band. Stephanie was beside us with her drumsticks, thrashing, thwacking, and attacking the imaginary drums around her to the rocking rhythm inside her head. Though she appeared laid back with a sense of humor, she was the pounding pulse and driving heartbeat of this band. Chris's steady rhythm on the Hammond kept us focused and the music tight. She was staring at something inside herself or meditating. I guess it was her way of dealing with being anxious or strung out because of the waiting, but I wanted to hear what was bothering her. She could be so lively or serious one moment, then so stand-offish and "I have to be alone" the next. Maybe

I was just jealous of the guy she was seeing, and I didn't want to admit it.

A knock sounded on the door, and when it opened, Ed entered and said, "All right, girls, it's time. Joe, Lou, and I will be backstage in the wings, keeping an eye on the dance floor in front of you. If we feel any animals are getting out of control and want to jump up on stage, we'll rush down and stand below in front of the stage. You have a big, lively crowd out there. And more people coming in. But the alcohol adds to the potential of the psychos growing crazy. Play your hearts out. Have fun. And do me and your uncles proud!"

Exclamations of "We will, Daddy!" and "Thanks, Dad!" came from Chris and Dawn, while, "Don't hurt anyone unless you have to!" was flung from Stephanie.

He left the door open, and Dawn, Stephanie, Chris, and I filed out. Ten feet up the hallway, we were walking leisurely past the room on our left where the band of "sexist pigs" were waiting to perform. Laughter shrieked inside from a girl, followed by the guys chuckling as bottles were clinking together, conjuring memories of my own alcoholic camaraderie that I was now so happy to walk away from.

Hurrying onto the stage where behind a heavy, black curtain was an unsettled, wild, rumbling roar of ferocious curiosity, Dawn and Stephanie were teasing and exciting it with the bass plucking at pounding beats dancing crazily to the exploding drums. Chris was slightly ahead of me when she stopped before stepping onto the stage and turned, reaching out to take my hand. With a slight smile, she asked, "Would you please say a prayer with me, Joey?" I was completely caught off guard. I never would've thought of that. She stared into my eyes tenderly, almost pleadingly. "Please, Joey? It can be a Hail Mary, Our Father, or something simple."

In a mounting, escalating volume, the crowd was chanting, "Pebbles! Pebbles! We want Pebbles!"

I said, "I'd love to. How about a Hail Mary?"

"Okay."

And we both bowed our heads. When we finished, Chris's eyes sparkled, embracing mine, and she smiled, gripping my hand, then let it go and casually strolled across the stage to her Hammond B-3 Organ. Staring after her, a soothing wave of feeling flowed through me as I felt this was what it meant to be close to someone. But I couldn't figure her out.

Walking up to my amp, I plugged my guitar into it while butterflies were stirring inside of me. But I was close to these songs. As I was making sure my Strat was tuned, I felt ready for the audience's reaction. My pantyhose were a little tight, but energy and adrenalin, and a lot of cotton that I stuffed in earlier, would override any annoying pinches to my testicles.

On stage, I was down and a little left of Stephanie, Dawn was across from me, and Chris was down and a little to Dawn's right. Then, as the right and left side of the curtain slid open, revealing us, the frame of the audience grew wider and deeper as its shouting and cheering grew thunderous. I glanced over at Dawn, and there was this wild, mesmerizing stare. She was like a statue, just standing there. Concern flashed in Chris's eyes, and I started to panic. *What is she doing!* Meanwhile, the deafening decibels of crazy, yelling, and clapping was beginning to subside to mumbling questions of concern and unease over Dawn's wellbeing. Out of the corner of my eye, stalwart Ed was slowly walking out on stage when Dawn calmly, and with purpose, confidently walked down to the apron of the stage carrying her bass guitar. Wanting her presence to demand silence in spite of an occasionally tossed, crude pick-up line or lewd comment flung at her on her sexy outfit arousing raucous laughter, the audience, oddly curious, was waiting for what she had to say. Nonchalantly, she knelt down facing a good-looking young man and asked him his name.

"Randy," he yelled, piercing the ceiling.

Thankfully, that was my cue to turn to Stephanie and nod. And the two of us began a more electrically charged, ardent, drum pounding rendition of Dawn's version of Rod Stewart's "Maggie May." '"Wake up, Randy, I think I got something to say to you..."' With her bass guitar hammering the beat, her rough passionate, and guttural voice sang to Randy as if they had been lovers forever. Randy stood mesmerized as if he genuinely believed Dawn wanted to be with him. He suddenly became very popular, as Dawn chose the right song, and attitude, for the audience's first impression to embrace us.

After the song, Chris introduced each of us.

"You girls don't have to sing or play! Just walk

around the stage! You look beautiful!" shouted a stocky, bearded guy who aroused laughter around him.

Someone else flung out, "Yeah! Put them guitars away and just dance!"

I walked over to Dawn and we agreed on the next song. She told Stephanie, and I told Chris. I turned toward Stephanie and counted, "One and two and three," and we burst into one of my songs. It was weird. Immediately people looked dazed as if they were thinking, *What are you guys playing? We don't know that song.* But shortly, as we kicked into the hook, then the chorus, I could see wide smiles, heads nodding, and bodies swaying and moving to the rhythm with hands clapping. And except for two more covers, we played my songs, and the audience gave us a cheering ovation as the curtains closed. Immediately, Ed, Joe, and Lou hurried on stage to get our equipment off as Wayside's crew ran on, getting their instruments, mikes, amps, etc., to set up.

I knew it was early, but while heading down the hallway, I was feeling such a phenomenal, natural high I couldn't believe I used to take drugs to get it. Abruptly, Chris yelled, "Dawn! What the hell were you doing?! Next time tell us you want to wait for the audience to be quiet before you do your thing with a guy. You had us all scared that something was wrong with you!"

"I'm sorry! But we never had such a huge crowd like that. I just wanted to do something dramatic to get their attention."

"Well, you did do that!" flung Stephanie over her shoulder.

We were sweating as we entered our room.

"Joey, take your wig off and get a towel to wipe your face," advised Chris. "Cool off. We don't go back on for almost two hours. I'll put fresh make-up on you before then."

A knock sounded, and Ed entered, smiling. "You're a hit! You're not what they expected, just playing covers and strutting your God given physiques around the stage. The original music surprised them. They like it! Joe, Lou, and I are going to be down on the dance floor closer to the stage for your next set. It's getting crazy out there, and guys are getting drunk and making even more lewd comments about you all. So, we're going to keep their sick fantasies off the stage."

"Thanks, Daddy," the girls said in unison.

"And Dawn! Please, give me a heads up before you ever do what you did out there again before such a large and unruly crowd!"

"Okay, Daddy. Sorry."

"Oh, Joey. People are really amazed by your guitar playing. Chris, Stephanie, Dawn, I hear people swearing you're *guys* dressed up as girls! That's how great you all play."

"What the—? Is that supposed to be a compliment?" asked Stephanie.

"Let's face it. We're the only girl band that has ever played in Baltimore," said Chris.

"Then, hell yeah! We'll take that as a great compliment," Dawn hollered.

"But they *are* unknowingly right about Donna," chuckled Stephanie.

"I'll be back to let you know when you're all on stage again," said Ed.

"Thanks, Dad!" the girls said together as Ed closed the door.

"Dawn," I said, "your base lines through the songs are pounding tight and right on."

"Thank you, Donna."

"And Stephanie, what you do with your base drum peddle, how you hit it and follow it with a quick half beat, really accentuates Dawn's bass during the songs. People don't want to stop dancing."

"Thanks. John Bonham of Zeppelin does it great, and I've been practicing to perfect it."

"You see, Donna," Dawn began, "after you left last night, we listened to your songs and we—"

"Wanted to take some liberties with creative inspiration," interjected Stephanie.

"You guys were practicing after I left?" I asked, shocked from a sucker punch by surprise.

"Yes. We wanted you to be proud of us!" said Chris, overjoyed.

"After hearing how you're playing out there, I am!" But no way could I imagine that Chris would continue to rehearse last night as upset as she was with me and as tired as she and her sisters acted before I left. So why didn't Chris tell me herself that they rehearsed? She seemed more and more like a puzzle to me. I couldn't figure her out.

"Let's rehearse just a few songs for the next set so you can hear my ideas on bass with them," said Dawn enthusiastically.

CHAPTER 17

While our instruments were being fired up on stage, waiting for the curtain to open to begin our second set, the audience was yelling loudly, "Pebbles rocks, Pebbles rocks," which made me chuckle at how appropriate our name was. We'd heard some of the previous band's set—Hardcore, the guys who were demeaning us earlier—and frankly, we weren't that impressed. Their musicianship was very good. However, the few original songs they played sounded bland: no passionate hooks, no melodies that blew me away with jealousy, or any engaging riffs. Just copycats in a lower or higher key with little impromptu variations of the melody in dance music of popular bands today. Therefore, we decided not to open with a cover but just keep the crowd anticipating what new song we would play next to excite their curiosity.

As the curtain was slowly parting and I was igniting the passion of the first song, suddenly, out of the corner of my eye, I saw a lean, dark, long haired mammal jump up onto the stage on my left. Standing tall after slowly getting up, he staggered toward me, shouting and slurring, "Donna, I'm Tim! I love you! I…. I just…."

As he was reaching his arms out to embrace me and getting closer, I started panicking and slowly moving backwards, looking where I could set my guitar down and hurry off the stage. He could seize me and claw his way all over my body, knocking my breasts out and taking my wig off. Dawn started walking over, and Stephanie was quickly coming around her drums to come to my aid as well. All the while, people were screaming, "Watch out!" "Get that guy!" and laughing when Lou shot toward the guy, grabbing him with a bear-hug and dragging him off the stage.

"Thank you, Uncle Lou!" chimed loudly from Dawn and Stephanie. I'd have to tell him afterwards or lose my femininity before the crowd. I took a few deep breaths to settle myself as Chris came over, laying her hand on my shoulder to ask if I was okay. That was thoughtful of her. I nodded that I was, and when she was seated at the organ, I turned to Dawn and Stefanie and bobbed my head to signal I was ready while the audience was clamoring, "Let's go, Pebbles! Let's go, Pebbles!"

Time felt like it was dragging during our second set, and I attributed it to us being more relaxed. It felt like our adrenaline was playing in the first set, and the performance was in fast forward mode. Still playing in harmony with each other, but fast. Definitely *now*, I could feel we were in the present, listening to the audience, hearing the passion, and seeing their bodies in various dancing contours reacting to it. I believe rehearsing and talking about the songs during the break made a big difference as well. I could hear the little nuances and tones that Chris and Dawn said they wanted to add during some of the songs, and they sounded great. Stephanie was keeping the pounding pulse that aroused the crowd's excitement and interest. And I noticed while we were playing, fewer people were dancing. Many were flowing toward the stage to listen and enjoy our musicianship. *And yes*, to go gaga over our bodies! But it seemed to me I was staring at more nodding heads that were mesmerized and thrilled by the music.

Unfortunately, but thankfully, the time came for Ed, Joe, and Lou to realize it was necessary to implement marine-style crowd control. Their hefty physiques loomed along the perimeter of the stage, where before them, in the center of the crowd, was evolving a bulge of drunken guys shouting crazily, "We want Pebbles! We want Pebbles!" Then suddenly, they charged in a wild, screaming surge, climbing over one another in a desperate attempt to jump up on the stage to manhandle us. Girls were screaming and shoving into others, scurrying out of their way. Thankfully, the robust and impregnable wall of brawn and defensive skills of Ed and his brothers repelled the intoxicated madness of attack. Meanwhile, maintaining our calm and keeping our faith in Ed and his brothers, we stayed focused on playing, and I was scanning individual faces in the audience to see how they were reacting to my music. Some were smiling while their heads were bobbing, some had their body moving and gyrating to the rhythm, and some were even jumping up and down and clapping. Then others seemed to have eyes planted on us, pointing at one of us as if impressed with how we were playing and commenting to the person beside them.

Suddenly, Dawn called over to me and said, "Donna, that's our last song!" And the curtain started closing. That fast, and it was over.

But the clapping hands and foot stamping were growing thunderous. Then, shouting began erupting in the audience. "No! No! Don't Go! Hell No! Don't Go!" was rippling louder from the front of the stage to the back of the club. After the curtain closed, Dawn and I had taken off our guitars, and Chris was going over to help Stephanie pack up her drums when a tall Italian man who must've been in his forties, with a slight paunch, thick, jet-black, neatly styled hair just below his ears, and wearing a blazing blue polyester suit, approached us and said in a rough and gravelly voice, not unlike Marlon Brando's character in The Godfather, "Hi, my name's Anthony. You girls played great!" with a beaming smile across his face. "What a surprise youse all turned out to be! The audience loves your music! Hear that? I want youse all to come back here soon!" he emphasized, flashing gold rings on fingers stretching out to embrace us. "You'll hear from me. And I just talked to your father and uncles. How about playing an encore song and then calling it a night, okay?"

"Sure," Chris said.

"All right. Beautiful. I'll see youse all again."

As Anthony was leaving, I said, "Chris, what song are we going to play? We played all the songs we rehearsed."

"Dawn, Stephanie, and I know it. You will, too, when you hear it. We've rehearsed it. Don't worry."

Chris returned to her B3, Stephanie to her drums, and as Dawn and I were retrieving our guitars, I asked her the name of the song. She smiled, saying, "You'll know it. A good song to end the night on."

As I walked over to position myself and play what I didn't know I had rehearsed, which bothered me since I was a perfectionist, the curtain was slowly pulling apart. Briefly, we stood dumbfounded while witnessing the resounding clapping, the detonation of stamping feet, and the booming chanting of "One more song! One more song!"

Suddenly, Stephanie hammered her drumsticks in beat three times, and on the fourth beat, Chris began the song in a slow tempo of a melody that sounded familiar. Then, along with Dawn's bass pounding a rhythm gently that kept reinforcing to me why I should know this song, I turned to Chris, who was smiling tenderly at me. The song was "Not Afraid of Being Close." My song! How?

Dawn was mouthing the words vehemently, "Start playing!" Nervously, hesitantly, I began playing. Then, *they aren't expecting me to sing, are they*? burst panic into my heart. Quickly I turned to Chris, who began singing. Thank God! I wouldn't have been able to. I'd be singing my most personal secret to myself in front of all these strangers. I'd be so embarrassed.

The crowd was becoming very quiet. I was so blown away that the girls wanted to stay up late and rehearse this song. I turned around and had to wipe my tears away, even if it was going to mess up my make-up. But it was the last song, anyway. Facing the crowd, I saw that they were calm, some couples dancing slowly. Others were just standing and gently swaying until, surprised by a pulsing bass and slashing guitar riff leading into the hook and chorus with blazing guitar, bass, and drums, all were briefly excited to dance, only to shortly slow down and join in each other's arms once again. It was so cool and amazing to see this song come alive. The girls did a great job on it.

When it was over, there was an explosion of applause, sending a wave of the crowd's appreciation crashing over us, and I stood mesmerized, drowning contentedly in the excitement. "Joey, let's go!" shouted Chris, grabbing me by the arm and yanking me back into consciousness.

Ed, Joe, and Lou had already jumped up on the stage and started gathering our equipment as I followed Chris, Stephanie, and Dawn off stage left. Two guys and the girl in Hardcore, who had been standing in the wings, were walking on stage toward us.

"Wow, girls! You rocked!" flung one of the guys passing by.

"Hey, hang out! We'll go out for a drink afterwards!" said the other.

"Sorry, we got a gig on the block where we just

strut around naked on stage, not knowing how to play the guitar," said Dawn sarcastically in a ditzy caricature of a dumb blonde.

"What?!" stared the guy in shock. "I thought—"

"Serves you right, Ricky," said the girl, snickering and joining the other guy, going upstage to get their equipment and set it up.

One cute guy with blond, curly hair coiling down his shoulders stepped in front of me and said, "My name's George. You girls were great. But darling, the way you played that Strat sent chills up and down my body. Why don't we—?"

"Donna has laryngitis. And she's too busy with us to jam with you," Chris said with a forced smile, pulling me away.

"Thanks for rescuing me," I chuckled.

During the ride home, the girls were laughing and teasing me about being too shocked to start playing my song once Chris surprised me by playing it. "I completely forgot that I included it with the songs I gave you. I'm just glad I gave it to you with the revisions I made on it."

"Well, girls, I made several tapes of your performances tonight," said Ed. "A couple of men said they were managers or an agent and wanted a tape, but I gave them my phone number instead. You have to get that music copyrighted, Joey. Some other people and I also exchanged numbers, and one fellow said he'd call me about hiring you guys for a gig at a bar in Georgetown and The Marble Bar in Baltimore."

"The Marble Bar, Dad? That is legit. An up and coming club for new bands," Dawn said eagerly.

I was thinking I'd been away so long I didn't know any of the popular clubs. But after what I'd been through with my band, I didn't get excited anymore with what any manager or agent said until a lawyer read it and said, "Sign it." Otherwise, in my mind, there were business people who only wanted to exploit your naiveté and eagerness, waiting to sign you to a record deal to capitalize on your hard work and talent. Then, like me, they'd leave you dreamless, brokenhearted, and desperate.

"Daddy, did we look sexy enough on stage?" asked Dawn, giggling.

"Would your uncles and I be wrestling with drunken idiots wanting to jump on stage and heaving them back into the crowd all night if you weren't?"

said Ed sarcastically, obviously irritated. "I'm talking to your mother, and you girls are turning the heat down on those costumes."

"Oh, Daddy. We've argued about this before. Being sexy sells tickets," insisted Dawn.

"Well, not after tonight. What your uncles and I heard from people in the audience is that your music sold you. So, those costumes are history! Subject closed."

"Oh, Daddy, come on! All we're doing is having fun. Look at all the money we'll—"

"Quiet, Dawn!" snapped Chris. "Dad's right. We're not Barbie dolls. Joey has turned us into musicians. What that jerk from Hardcore said about us doesn't bother you?"

"Just because of what happened to you last year, you think that every—"

"Shut up, or I'll slap your face!" screamed Chris.

"Girls! Girls!" yelled Ed.

"Dawn, open your mouth, and I'll put my fist in it!" barked Stephanie.

"That's enough!" hollered Ed. "Joey, I don't blame you if you want to quit this band right now.

Being around catty, fighting girls all the time will drive you crazy!"

I was saved from having to respond to him because, living so close to The Palace, we were pulling into Chris's driveway.

Ed said, "All right, girls, outside, and hug and kiss your uncles and thank them for their physical prowess in protecting you all night."

"Daddy, we always do that," said Stephanie emphatically.

"I know. But tonight, they *earned* it!"

As we got out of the car, I wondered what it was that had happened to Chris last year. The chill in the night air scooted the girls over to hug their uncles, thank them for their help, and kiss them goodbye. I walked over behind them, and as the girls were turning away, I came up to their uncles, and one of them said, "Joey, you don't have to kiss us. We'll just shake hands," and we all laughed.

"Great job tonight, Joey," said Lou. "I heard a number of people say they were really amazed at how well you could play your guitar."

"And how sexy you looked," quipped Joe, and we laughed. "But seriously, Joey, other than manhandling a group of drunken idiots who wanted to charge up on stage, Ed, Lou, and I were very proud to witness how you helped change those girls into serious musicians. You all sounded…like professionals up there."

"Thank you. But those girls just needed some original songs to bring out their natural talent and creativity. And we wouldn't have made it out of there *alive* if it wasn't for you guys," I said, feeling relieved.

"That's where *we* come into play." And we all laughed.

They started unloading our equipment, and I entered the basement studio and heard, "I'm really sorry, Chris. But I never would've said anything about you and Mark."

Dawn was talking to Chris, and as Stephanie saw me, she said somewhat awkwardly, "Ah, hey, Joey. Why don't you sit down, and I'll help you take your makeup off, honey?"

Dawn and Chris then hugged each other, and as Dawn was leaving, she said, "Thank you, Joey, for an out-of-sight night. It was great. We can't wait to do it again."

"Yeah, me too. Good night, Dawn."

Stephanie carefully took my wig off, folded it, and put it in a plastic bag.

"Stephanie, go on upstairs. I can help Joey," Chris said.

"Joey, I am so high on feeling awesome in this dream come true. I don't know when I'll ever sleep again!" Stephanie shouted and gave me a hug and a kiss. "Goodnight. See you at our next rehearsal."

I said goodnight and told her I couldn't wait until we did it again as well.

Chris came over and grabbed some Kleenex, digging them into the Pond's Cold Cream Cleanser, and started wiping make-up off on the right side of my face and gently cleaning it while I started on my left side. Obviously, with her experience, she was quicker than my more conscientious and meticulous slowness. "I'm sorry you had to hear Dawn and I fighting on the way home. She works hard and is very dedicated. But she can be very stubborn at times. Especially when it's all about 'the look' of us in the band. She's very egotistical. And Stephanie and I are tired of it. We're both ready for some changes."

"Listening to your dad talk, he is too." An

uncomfortable pause suddenly intervened while Chris was cleaning the table and putting everything neatly away in drawers. Once I finished taking my make-up off and threw the tissues into the trash, I stood up, ready to change out of my costume. Chris had to know I'd heard Dawn talk to her about Mark as I entered the studio. However, it appeared she wasn't going to talk about it now. And frankly, I didn't blame her. It had been a long, stressful week, and I knew she was really tired after rehearsing late last night. I was tired.

"I'll change, and you can get to bed, Chris. I can let myself out."

"No. I'll go up and use the bathroom, wait for you to change, then I'll walk you out to the car. It's no big deal," she said blandly and matter-of-factly, walking toward the stairway.

No smile? No excitement about how we performed? What's wrong with her? Something is definitely eating at her! And I'm sure it concerns Mark. She probably wants to walk me outside to tell me about him. Maybe she is using me to be in her band. No, that can't be true. She never gave me any vibes to believe she wanted to be in a relationship with me. Though she certainly made

Grandma believe she liked me, with frivolous touch-feely kinds of signs that friends do to one another to appreciate their company or support. But definitely, no conversations on her part intimating how she felt for me. Just business to cement a possible, hard working relationship together. And this band was what I needed right now to get my confidence back, build my ego, and, most importantly, to earn some serious money.

Walking out to the car, Chris was quiet. I didn't want to say anything. I was just waiting to hear about her and Mark so I could stop thinking about wanting a relationship with her.

"Joey, were you upset that we...that I wanted to play 'Not Afraid of Being Close' without telling you?"

Wow. I was. And I wasn't. "Yes, and no," I said. "I was because I haven't told anyone why I wrote it. I even forgot that it was among the songs I gave you to rehearse. Then, hearing it performed on stage before an audience for the first time, I was so blown away. This *huge* wave of happy and sad emotions suddenly overwhelmed me. I was drowning in memories I wanted to forget. But then again, it's why I wrote the song. Ironic, isn't it?"

"I'm sorry I didn't tell you. I wanted to surprise you. But it was late, we were tired, I was upset with you, the way my sisters were playing, and — myself: from bad choices that keep tormenting me. But after you left Monday night, and even though we were all tired, Dawn and Stephanie didn't want to stop rehearsing. Some of your songs inspired them to want to add their own flair to them, as you heard tonight."

"And they sounded great."

"Then, when I played 'Not Afraid of Being Close' for them, they thought it was such a beautiful love song that we agreed to play it tonight and surprise you. And while looking at you, I could see that we did."

"You saw me wipe my tears away, huh?"

"I did," and a smile flitted across her face and sparkled in her eyes.

"Well, they were happy tears, too, watching people enjoy the song."

"Your song spoke to me and those in the audience, Joey. And to everybody who's ever been hurt in a relationship."

I didn't know what to say, and *the* inevitable awkward pause came between us when suddenly I felt compelled to share with her, even though she was seeing Mark, why this song was so special to me. So, I began telling her about my relationship with Kay.

She listened so intently with her eyes riveted upon mine. When I finished, she said very seriously while tenderly stroking my cheek, "I understand, Joey. Believe me."

Not wanting her pity, I simply said, "I'm glad you suggested we say a prayer together. I felt more relaxed afterwards."

"I did too. Other guys would've thought that weird. Thank you," she said with a grin.

"You know, living with my grandmother, going to church, meeting you, being in your band, the audience enjoying my music—if that's what happens when I had nothing before I started praying, then I'll enjoy being weird. I have to tell Dawn and Stephanie thanks for their hard work in staying up late to rehearse those songs."

Our eyes seemed to reach out to each other. In spite of Mark, I wanted to kiss her with so much tenderness and feeling, but I didn't dare face rejection and hearing about Mark after exposing my agony from writing a song on rejection. Best to just keep our relationship as friends.

"You and your family enjoy your Thanksgiving, Chris. And I'll call you over the weekend when you want to rehearse again."

"Joey...." Her face looked like she was struggling to tell me something. *Here it comes Mark!* "What do you think about the managers who were interested in us and took Dad's phone number?"

"When — *if* — they call, and *if* we get a gig and are paid what we deserve, I'll think they might be legit, and I'll wait to see what'll happen next."

"Boy, why do you sound so pessimistic at times?" Frowning, I gazed up at the stars. "What's bothering you, Joey? We played really well tonight. People who heard us before said they couldn't believe we were the same band. And it was because of you."

"I don't mean to be a downer, Chris, but I've been through this before. And until we get somebody who'll work hard for us and keep getting us good paying jobs, playing alongside of other good bands at respectable venues outside of Maryland, then we'll just keep being a popular local band." The stars again tugged my attention toward them. "I always wanted to connect the dots up there of what I'd look like when I achieved my goal." I chuckled self-consciously. "My own constellation. Never been able to, though. But meeting you has been better than that. A wonderful surprise—a gift." Our eyes held one another. "Goodnight, Chris," I said, turning away and getting into the car. I didn't give a damn about Mark—I just had to share how I felt about her. She walked away from the car with a faint smile, stopped, and slowly raised her hand to wave goodbye.

Driving home, I couldn't stop wondering what it was that Chris was going through with Mark. Then I chuckled when a burst of self-conceit flashed before me, believing she was struggling over whether she wanted a relationship with me instead of Mark. Seriously, however, I couldn't stop wondering why Chris was so unhappy with herself.

CHAPTER 18

I came back to Grandma's around one in the morning. She had fallen asleep listening to the radio again in her bedroom, and the rosary was resonating clearly from behind the closed door. I had a lot to be thankful for since I arrived at Grandma's house. I slid down the wall, leaning against it while saying some of the rosary. I thanked God for motivating the girls to work hard for the band being successful tonight and for the audience liking my music. I asked Him to help Chris overcome whatever was troubling her so she could be happy, and if it was His plan that I could be happy with her. I also asked Him to help Grandma's arthritis in her knees heal and to keep my mom safe and happy and not let my dad hurt her.

Then, I quietly entered Grandma's room and turned the radio off. Heading to my own room, I took a shower and in bed, said some of the prayers out of the book of daily prayers Grandma had given me.

In the morning, my eyes opened to shimmering white cotton curtains with blue flowers sewn upon them on the window across from me. The small box-shaped electric clock on the little table beside my bed with orange numbers glared nine o'clock. Immediately, the clanging of pots, pans, and ceramic bowls clamored like an alarm, indicating that it was time to get up and help Grandma prepare the Thanksgiving Day meal. Briefly, the high I was riding from last night's standing ovation, thundering applause, stamping of feet, and yelling of "One more song" held me down, grinning in ecstasy. I was envisioning a huge crowd waiting for us at our next gig, then surging toward us as we got out of our limo. It was exciting and funny. I could just lay there and plan how I'd like to see my future unfold before me.

But staring around my room, reality seeped in, sobering me. Where was the publicity to keep this dream going? The money to keep the momentum going with better exposure and more popular places to play? And, of course, a bigger paycheck for playing at these places? On that enthusiastic and depressing downer, I swept the blankets off me and got out of bed, took my jeans off the chair across from the bed, and jumped into them. Taking my deodorant off the bureau, I swiped it beneath my arms, pulled on a long-sleeved wool shirt that Grandma had thankfully laid on the bench at the end of the bed, and finally slipped into Granddad's slippers that were beneath it. In the bathroom, I turned on the cold water, cupped my hands under the faucet, filled them with cold water, and splashed my face and eyes repeatedly to rouse me, facing the present.

Finally, I entered the kitchen to begin the day helping Grandma. She was kneeling on the floor, rummaging through her bottom cabinet, looking for something. "There you are, you little bugger." She brought out a certain size pot.

"Good morning, Grandma."

"Joey! You gave me a scare," she said, turning to me and chuckling.

"I'm sorry, Grandma." I bent over, helping her up.

"I figured you'd get in late last night." Taking

my hand, her face grimaced in pain as she groaned, "It can be easy going down, Joey. But I need something to grab onto to help myself up."

"Well, I'm here for you, Grandma. So, just ask me if you need anything."

"I'm glad you slept in, Joey. I bet you were tired."

"I was. I slept like a rock. And it felt good."

"You have breakfast. Then I wanna hear all about it," she said, arranging pots, pans, knives, and a cutting board on the counter and bringing vegetables out of the refrigerator.

I didn't realize how hungry I was until I started eating. I had four eggs and four slices of scrapple. I knew it was because I had been so nervous yesterday and had hardly eaten anything — probably one of the reasons I was so tired. Once I finished, washed the dishes, and put them away, Grandma and I sat down at the Formica table, and I began my story with me having to dress as a girl.

From that moment on, the whites of her eyes grew wide, and her smile even wider. She couldn't stop exclaiming and squealing with pure, delightful joy every few moments, "Oh, Joey!" "And the owner said he wants us to come back and play again."

"Is that right? Ah, Joey. And the whole time, you were a girl! Holy cow, if that don't beat all! Gosh, I would've loved to have seen that. I seen on *The Jackie Gleason Show* and *The Red Skeleton Show*, men dressed up as women, and they were funny. Tell me, are you going to see Chris again?" she asked, with eyes beaming in anticipation.

"After Thanksgiving. We've been working so hard this week that she wants to relax and spend time with her family." And that was partly true.

"Oh, that's good, Joey," her smile said excitedly. "Just let me know what night will be good, so I can fix you two a nice dinner."

"I'll look forward to it, Grandma." I didn't believe it was going to happen, but I wasn't going to take that smile away from her.

Grandma was getting up, and I saw her face grimace in pain. "Are you all right?"

"It's just my knees, Joey."

"Don't forget to remind me to remind you to take you to your doctor's appointment next Tuesday," I chuckled.

"Joey, hon, the pain will not let me forget," she

said, walking over to the stove. "And Pat also wrote the number down and put it with my medications. Here you are, Joey. This is a list of what we'll need for dinner tomorrow."

The A&P was only three minutes from Grandma's house in the Westview Mall on Route Forty, but with Thanksgiving being tomorrow, people were packed in there like sardines, crowding every aisle and standing in long lines at the cashiers. What would normally have been a ten-minute shopping errand ended up lasting an hour and twenty minutes. Grandma was even surprised at how long I was gone.

"Boy, Joey, it never used to be like that." I was taking the groceries out of the bags, and she said, "Oh, Joey, your mother called a little while after you left. She wanted to wish you a Happy Thanksgiving and said she and your dad are fine and visiting friends. She said she loves you, and, if she gets a chance, will call again tomorrow. They'll be home early next week. I told her you were in a band, and she was excited for you. I said nothing about you being dressed up as a girl. I wanted you to tell her that."

I thanked her and, while putting the groceries away, thought about not seeing Mom for over two years. Then a pang of sadness slugged me. That first couple of months I was away, she would cry on the phone and tell me to come home or to call more often. I couldn't. Being on the road, I didn't see a payphone or didn't have money to call. She wanted to send me money from her job working in a doctor's office, but I said no, I was doing fine, even though a lot of times I wasn't. One time I called, and Mom started crying because she missed me. Then, I heard Dad yell at her in his callous voice, "He's making choices necessary to pursue his dream. I sure as hell never took the chance! And if he succeeds, great. If not, he comes home, goes to school, gets an office job, gets married, and is miserable for the rest of his life!" When I did call, it was in between long intervals. When she wasn't home, I'd leave a message telling her I loved her very much and Dad too. Even though it was very hard to love Dad. Those were times I was feeling very depressed and wanted so much to hear her pleading urge begging me to come home. Would I? No. But I wanted her nurturing love so very much. Then, when I met Kay, I didn't want to be separated from her. We were living a dream of love. I *never* anticipated the sudden nightmare. Now, with Chris — it was starting all over again. But I at least knew about Mark. And she seemed to be struggling with her feelings for him. Or his for her. But I was stronger now and wouldn't let what I couldn't control spiral me down into a deep self-destructive depression like last time. Now, I could walk away. After last night, I was confident my music would make me successful wherever I went.

"Joey, open these cans of string beans and pour them in this colander in the sink to drain, please," Grandma said, pulling me back into the present.

"Sure, Grandma."

We spent close to three hours prepping and cooking. When I was young and stayed over at Grandma's for the weekend, I'd watch her cook big meals for family get-togethers, like a birthday or a holiday, or just if Mom felt like coming over for a Sunday visit. It looked easy. And fun. No way! Standing in one place for a long time, cutting, peeling, or stirring something over the hot stove for ten minutes or more, was hard. No wonder Grandma — and Mom, when once in a while she'd cook dinner for guests coming over — would feel tired afterwards. And why they expected me to eat everything put on my plate.

It amazed me that Grandma knew exactly how many dishes she could make and stuff into the refrigerator. We had room for one more dish, and that was going to be her signature dessert of mincemeat pie that I would help her prepare by rolling out the pie crust. There would also be a coconut cake.

"You hungry, Joey?" she asked nonchalantly.

"Sure, Grandma."

"All right. Let's have a grilled cheese over ham sandwich with a slice of tomato. Or would you rather just have bacon instead of ham?"

"No, ham is fine," I said, cleaning off the table. But I said I'd have lettuce instead of a tomato. I preferred tomatoes in tomato sauce and couldn't eat a tomato by itself.

Grandad could never understand why I didn't love tomatoes. Everyone he knew loved tomatoes. But every year, when school let out in early June, Mom would take me down to stay at Grandma's on a Friday to spend the weekend helping Grandad turn over the dirt in his vegetable garden and fertilize it so he could plant over twenty tomato plants. Then he'd give me ten dollars for helping him.

After lunch, the turkey was the last thing to prepare. Grandma always bought a fresh turkey for Thanksgiving. She took out the neck and wrapped gizzards, and rinsed the turkey under the faucet. The gizzards she would cook and give to the neighbor's cat. She brushed melted butter on the turkey and afterwards shook her seasonings all over it so the flavors would seep into the turkey while being in the refrigerator downstairs overnight.

"Now, I'll get up early tomorrow and fix the stuffing and shove it into the turkey and let it cook for four to five hours," Grandma said. "Are you ready to help me with the pumpkin pie and coconut cake, Joey?"

I had completely forgotten about them as I began yawning and feeling drowsy. But I said, "I'm ready when you are," hoping she'd postpone that until tomorrow as well. She didn't, and like the hard and dedicated worker she was, we spent the next two and a half hours preparing the ingredients and baking one more pie and the cake. I learned that baking was very methodical, with a lot of careful measuring—and patience! But more importantly, watching Grandma, I knew it was love.

I noticed she was limping more than usual, especially when she was standing a lot. Once she put the pies in the oven, I told her to take a shower and that I'd use the timer and watch the pies in the oven, clean up, take the pies out, then put the cake in the oven.

"Ah, Joey, that would be great. Thank you, honey," she said, smiling.

I watched her hobbling across the kitchen, then she frightened me when she paused to get her balance by holding onto the doorframe.

I hurried over to take her arm. "You hold onto me, Grandma, and we'll walk together." I put my arm around her, and we walked slowly to her bedroom.

"Thank you, Joey. I'll be fine now," she said as I walked her into her bedroom and helped her sit down on her comfortable upholstered armchair. "I'll just rest a minute, then take a shower and go to bed," she said slowly, catching her breath at intervals."

"Okay, Grandma," I said, feeling worried about her. "If you need anything, call me. Otherwise, I'll see you bright and early to put the turkey in the oven."

"All right, honey. Don't stay up too late."

"I won't."

I was cleaning up the kitchen, so I wouldn't have to do so much after the pie and cake were done, and the phone rang. That's Mom, I thought excitedly while walking to the phone. "Hello!"

"Hi, Joey. This is Chris."

Whoa! What a surprise. "Hi, Chris. How are you?"

"Really tired."

"From last night still?"

"No, from helping my mom cook all day!"

I chuckled. "That's exactly how I feel from helping my grandmother. In fact, she was so tired I just helped her to bed. But I must say I am proud of myself for learning how to make pie crusts from scratch."

"Joey, that's exactly what I was doing!" she laughed.

"Well, you at least had your sisters to help," I said.

"No, I didn't. They went out with friends."

"Why didn't you join them?"

"Because I couldn't let Mom cook and fix everything by herself. She always does. Dad will help for a little while. He'll open some cans, pour them in a pot, stir a little while, and wash some dishes, but he's in bed around eight o'clock every night. He'll get up at four o'clock every morning to work out to start his day, so he'll prepare the turkey. So, I can't be too hard on him."

"Well, look at it this way. You and I are preparing for our second calling if music doesn't pan out for us."

"You want to be a chef?"

"Not a chef, but I love sweets enough to want to learn how to bake them."

"I can't tolerate the standing for so long and the cutting, stirring, and cleaning," she said pitifully, and I had to laugh. "What's so funny?"

"I was complaining to myself about that all day."

She started laughing again. "I called because I wanted to ask you if I could come over and talk to you tomorrow after you have dinner. And sometime before you have dessert. If that's okay."

Whoa. That sounds ominous, I thought.

"Sure. Why don't you just come over and have dessert? That way, you can taste my pie or coconut cake and tell me what you think. Say around four o'clock?"

"Okay. That sounds good. Thank you."

"Ah, is it good news or bad news?" I asked, realizing I'd pretty much been preparing my psyche for the worst, knowing it was going to be about her and Mark. And, being that Thanksgiving ushered in the holidays, Mark had probably gotten his act together, and they'd talked, and everything was better between them.

"It's a little good news and some *not* good news. We're also changing the name of the band."

"Wonderful. I was hoping you'd think of changing it with me in it now."

"Yeah. We want people to respect us as musicians. We're thinking of names now. So, if you have any ideas, let us know."

"I will. Ah, I never heard of 'a *little* good' news and '*some* not good' news. It's either good or bad."

"I'll tell you tomorrow."

"I can't wait until tomorrow! Now I won't be able to sleep," I said in mock frustration.

"Then think of something good that happened to you today. Did you have a good laugh? Did you hug your teddy bear?"

I burst out laughing in spite of myself. "No, that's not going to work with me, Chris."

She started laughing. "I'll see you tomorrow at four. Bye." She hung up.

I was pretty sure the bad news would be about Mark. Fine. It wasn't like Chris and I had been dating, sharing our dreams and goals together, or worse, talking about a serious commitment and wanting to live with each other. We only just met. But being in a bad relationship with Mark right now, when her band just got good reviews, and with school on her mind and having to work part-time, she just may feel overwhelmed. I got it. She knew I liked her. And that was why she was struggling with how to tell me about Mark. She didn't want to hurt our relationship working together in the band. Maybe. But then—who knows? It was funny, though, how Chris and I thought alike at times. But I was young, and I would meet someone else.

I took a shower, and when I came out, I didn't hear the radio on in Grandma's bedroom. She must've been so tired she went straight to bed. I sat on my bed and decided to set the alarm for seven-thirty. I picked up the prayer book and read a few prayers, then I said some of the rosary. I asked God to bless our Thanksgiving tomorrow and to help Grandma's knees heal, and not to let her have a heart attack. I also prayed to ask God to help me find love in a relationship.

CHAPTER 19

The alarm blared loudly. I kept hitting the top of it, hoping to hit the snooze button, but after five times, I realized there must not be one where I was hitting it. So I forced myself to get up and just turn the alarm off.

I was greeted by the clanging of cutlery while going to the bathroom. Grandma was already up. I dressed and greeted her in the dining room, where she was setting the table.

"Joey, I thought you'd want to sleep awhile. You were working so hard helping me last night."

"Thanks, Grandma, but I should be helping you get that turkey in the oven. I'll go down and bring it up while you turn the oven on."

"Okay. I already have the stuffing made. While the oven's preheating, I'll stuff the turkey. Then you can help me put it in the oven, Joey."

"Okay. How early did you get up to make the stuffing, Grandma?"

"Six o'clock. I have a million things yet to do, Joey."

I chuckled to myself. A million things. But I had to admit while helping her prepare everything for today when I was young, and we came over to Grandma's house for Thanksgiving, I would never have had an idea of how much time and work went into fixing everything.

After I ate breakfast, I went into the dining room to see if Grandma needed any help.

"Joey, take out...." She paused and counted each place setting on the table. "Bring out five of my best plates of china and put them on the table for me, please."

"Oh, Grandma. Chris called last night, and I invited her over for dessert."

"Oh, Joey, that's great. I'll look forward to seeing her. I'll set a place for her for dessert and coffee."

"Thanks."

While I was setting the plates in their respective place settings on the table, Grandma was bending over, pulling bottles of whiskey, bourbon, sour mix, vodka, and gin out of the bottom of her corner cabinet, and placing them on top of the oak buffet across from the table. I had to laugh to myself because the labels on those bottles were faded, and the liquor in them had to be as old as me. But I'd never forget that Grandma always prided herself on making a batch of whiskey sours on the holidays and offering a glass to everybody as soon as they entered the kitchen. There she would remain until dinner was ready, then she and my aunts would bring all the dishes out to set on the dining room table. I was glad she remembered to have me buy a new bottle of sour mix. Her whiskey sours were potent. You could tell which of my aunts and uncles enjoyed them the most because during the afternoon and evening, their conversations were always cheerfully louder than the rest of us. Everybody left Grandma's house feeling happy and content.

I put on the Macy's Day Parade but only sat briefly for a few moments or grabbed a glimpse while flitting here and there, getting something that Grandma had forgotten to put on the dining room table or helping her do something in the kitchen. There was always something that had to be done. I never remembered my mother or the parents of friends who let me stay over right before a holiday ever taking this much time to decorate and prepare for any special dinner. Then suddenly, I realized sadly that I was probably experiencing firsthand the dying tradition of how Grandma's generation approached whatever they did with conscientious attention to detail and with love.

I emptied the trash from the kitchen and put it outside in the trash can beside the back porch. It felt good not to be living in the city anymore. I enjoyed inhaling the fresh air deeply while staring out across the graveyard behind Grandma's house, admiring the blazing, crayon colors of the autumn leaves. It was warm in the sun and pleasantly cool. White clouds glided across the ocean of blue above me, with gray mountains of clouds jutting up along the horizon in the north. A burst of wind slammed into the graveyard, shaking the leaves of the towering trees and hissing through the tall pines bordering each neighbor's property. I always loved the smell of pine trees during this time of year. Then a rush of wind scooted by me, smacking my face with a brisk chill. A perfect Thanksgiving Day.

It was time to pick up Grandma's friends. She wrote down the directions, and they all lived within five to ten minutes of her house. Jeanine and Lorine each used a cane while holding onto my arm, walking out of their first-floor apartment in Catonsville. Rose lived several blocks down from St. Agnes Church behind Samuel Ready School on Stanford Road, about two blocks off Route Forty, in a row house with steps and no railings. That scared me. Luckily, there was a back alley. I drove around to her fenced-in backyard and parked beside the gate. From her back door, there was only a step down onto a small porch, then one step down to a straight cement walkway to my car. She was small and frail, though very spry, and clutched my arm tightly, saying to me every other step, "Don't rush. Don't rush now."

Once we arrived back at Grandma's, I backed into the driveway, and two husky men in their forties approached me on the driver's side, saying, "You must be Joey. I'm Al, and this is Spike. We're here to help you escort the ladies into Mrs. Drexler's house."

Boy, was I surprised! I only expected help to bring the ladies out of Grandma's house. Now I could relax, knowing there was help getting them in the house too. Big smiles and "Oh Nina!" were exclaimed with surprise once those ladies entered Grandma's kitchen and were offered a whiskey sour, bourbon and water, or an old-fashioned. I lifted the roasting pan out of the oven, with the turkey tossing its savory smells throughout the room toward the "oohs and ahhs" of the ladies, who said regretfully that it had been years since they had been out of their homes for Thanksgiving. It brought tears to Grandma's eyes, and as I was lifting the turkey to the platter, my eyes were watering as well, seeing her so happy.

I was nearly finished carving the turkey when I heard the ladies asking for another drink. "Nina, did you make these whiskey sours? You must've been a barmaid in your youth. They're so good."

"Well, I used to experiment on Harry. When our children were young, he became very familiar with the neighborhood bars on our street, Bentlau, off Pratt. Many a night, I'd corner a friend of his to help me bring him home," she said, not a little perturbed.

"Oh, I know the area well, Nina. Pig Town, where we lived. My Vernon was a well-known patron at The Pigs in A Blanket Tavern on the corner of Pratt and Cross Street. But once I gave birth to our first child, I laid down the law, and we moved to the Uptown Apartments across from Edmondson Village."

And so, gradually, camaraderie took each by the hand, and they slowly made their way to the dinner table, where laughter never stopped and the conversation never ceased reminiscing about their past. I sat down and began passing vegetables, a plate of sliced turkey, cranberry sauce, gravy, etc., across the table and got up maybe twice to get Lorine and Rose another old-fashioned and Jeanine a couple of whiskey sours. Boy, those ladies could down'em! Finally, I was able to stay seated and enjoy what was on my plate. But not really. While eating, I found myself wanting to listen to the funny, sad, and tragic stories that each lady was relating about their families and how they survived through the Great Depression and two world wars. I was mesmerized. I never witnessed four women sitting together who could shed so many tears through laughter and sadness at the same time. Grandma's large cotton napkins sure came in handy.

Around three-thirty, I started clearing the table and preparing it for dessert, while I noticed intervals of silence but smiles of feeling content and at ease being here. And that made me happy because that was just what Grandma wanted today. I never thought cleaning up after dinner would be as active as fixing dinner. I didn't stop moving. I brought out the coffee pot, cream and sugar, four cups and saucers, spoons, forks, dessert plates, two pies, and the coconut cake.

"Joey, please sit down. I'll slice and serve the cake and pies."

"No, Grandma. I can do it. You relax."

"You hear that, Nina? Relax. Joey, in the short time I've known your grandmother, I know she does not know the meaning of the word," said Jeanine, chuckling.

As soon as all the ladies had their dessert and coffee before them, I was ready to sit down when the doorbell rang. Chris! I opened the door, and as soon as Chris entered, a rush of "Oooh" blew toward us.

"Who's this very pretty girl?" said Lorine.

"What's your name, honey?" asked Rose.

"Chris," she said, smiling.

"Are you Joey's friend?" asked Lorine.

Chris smiled, and her eyes turned to me. "I hope so." Everybody chuckled.

"That was cute," said Jeanine.

Chris came over and hugged Grandma, wishing her a happy Thanksgiving. Then she went around shaking hands with her friends, saying "Happy Thanksgiving" while each lady introduced herself to Chris, then turned, smiling toward the other, nodding their approval of Chris's polite etiquette.

"We're going to sit on the back porch, Grandma," I said.

"You both go right ahead. We'll be fine," said Grandma.

"Joey, honey," said Jeanine, a little louder due to possibly one too many old-fashioneds. "Go over and tell Spike that Jeanine would like him to come over and have a drink with her!" And a raucous laugh burst out from her, followed by the other ladies' laughter.

"For that matter, ask Al as well," chuckled

Lorine.

"Joey, you and Chris just sit on the back porch and enjoy yourselves. Lorine and Jeanine can see them in their dreams," Rose said, followed by an eruption of laughter around the table.

CHAPTER 20

Outside, the wind was brisk and revitalizing. The sun's gleaming, yellow-orange brightness was moving toward the horizon in front of the house, but its radiance angled such brilliance upon the myriad of colored leaves rising up like towering pompoms in the graveyard.

Chris sat down on a cushioned metal chair with arms, laid back in the chair comfortably, and inhaled deeply the lovely sight of the graveyard before her. She smiled and said, "I love your grandmother, Joey. She is so...so happy and content. And her friends are funny. I hope I am that funny at their age."

"During dinner, after hearing some of their happy and tragic stories over the years, I can only think that their laughter was what must've kept them alive for so long." I asked Chris how her Thanksgiving was, and she said it was fun listening to her sisters talk about the different kinds of lines guys had used to pick them and their friends up at some of the bars in Fells Point last night. "And my grandparents congratulated us and were excited to hear how our music lessons might finally be paying off for us after all these years, and especially for my parents. Which, by the way, is the good news I want to tell you."

Good? I thought. *That means Mark must be the bad.*

"My father said a man named Bill Zacchie called. He said he'd like to be our manager but wants to prove himself worthy first. He got us two gigs. The first on New Year's Eve at The Marble Bar in Baltimore, and the second two weeks later at the Nine-Thirty Club in D.C."

"Wow! I heard Stephanie say The Marble Bar was very good. But I haven't heard of the Nine-Thirty Club."

"It's a very hot venue for new bands to develop a following while travelling up the east coast to New

York. So things are looking pretty good so far, don't you think?" she said with a smile and a playful jab to my shoulder.

I nodded pensively. "It's a good start. But we'll need to get as many gigs as possible so we can develop a large following and show Bill we deserve bigger places to play outside of Maryland for a steady paycheck with more money." I wanted to sound happy, but I had to be a realist.

"What does it take to get you excited when there are signs telling you to be happy?"

"When the sign says sign the contract," I said, wanting to sound humorous and not glum.

Chris burst out laughing. "Why is it you come off so serious and yet have this underlying sense of humor?"

I stared out toward the graveyard. "I just have been around people for too long who haven't taken their craft or themselves seriously. It scares me that music is all I am, and people I know have graduated from college and are making a future for themselves, and I don't even have a car, a job, or a place to call my own."

"But you know who you are, Joey, while there

are many people, regardless of their age or income, who don't. They'll appear suave and confident to ignore their laziness or indifference to life and gorge their pleasure and selfishness off others regardless of how much they hurt them."

Chris paused. She was staring very intently inside of herself at what could've been hearsay or what could've been from actual experience. Or maybe from having to tell me what was going to hurt me: Mark.

I felt a change of scenery might be good for both of us. I would need to walk and look around me while hearing about him. "Can we take a walk, Chris? I've been standing and sitting most of the day, and I have to move."

She breathed deeply and turned to me with eyes slightly red and dewy. "Good idea," she said, forcing a smile. That look was ominous.

We rose and walked across Grandma's property toward the graveyard as I wondered if she was feeling okay. I said, "I love this graveyard with the woods surrounding it. This is the best time of year to walk around it."

"It is beautiful. There's also a small park on

several acres of land, with asphalt paths through forests, beside St. Christopher's school about a mile from us that I walk around occasionally," she said. Turning away from me, sniffling, she gazed at the tall oak, maple, and linden trees whose brilliant jewels of leaves were sparkling in the late afternoon fall sun's radiant russet and copper rays.

"I'm sorry, but I can't wait any longer," I blurted out, not wanting to hear her crying while saying she couldn't see me other than while in the band. "I need to know what the bad news is."

A chuckle burst from her. "I'm quitting the band next year after I graduate from Catonsville Community College. Then I'm transferring to Towson State to go into education. I want to teach music to children. I've only told my mother. Not my sisters or my father."

Whoa! Well, I was glad it wasn't what I expected. Unless she wanted to save it for later.

I was mulling over what she said as we were walking quietly and entering the graveyard. Then I said, "Good decision." I couldn't believe I said it so nonchalantly.

"What? That's weird. I thought you'd say that.

Why?"

"Because when I was dressed as Donna, and I could feel proud for writing the music, and I had practiced hard my whole life to know I was worthy to be on that stage, I felt I was only being appreciated for my looks and was being violated in every guy's mind who was staring at me with his tongue hanging out. And I know your father, you, and Stephanie want to change the costume we're wearing, but that still won't change how guys will see you in their minds. And I don't think you have the personality to perform in front of that."

A gray pall dropped over the graveyard as a cloud drifted by, blocking the sun. Suddenly, Chris was sniffling and sobbing.

I stopped and turned to her. "Chris, I didn't mean to hurt your feelings. I'm probably wrong and should've kept my mouth shut. If you stay focused on feeling and playing the music, you can ignore it."

"No. That's exactly how I feel. A little more than a year ago, before we started performing in clubs, I used to think I was cocky and cool for being a musician. Then I met this cute guy, Mark. He was as talented as you, in a band, and could have any girl he wanted — but he chose me. So, we hung out, went to parties, drank — he did drugs, but I didn't. But I tried them. I got pregnant, and he laughed. He said to just get rid of it, and we'd keep having fun. He lied to me and was seeing other girls. He was such a phony. Knew the right things to say to make me feel special and talented. And smart enough to convince me to follow what everyone else was doing and believing while I was denying my own values and faith."

Abruptly the tears just drained from her as she hurried out of the graveyard and stopped at Grandma's property line, too overwhelmed to continue any further. I came up behind her and took out one of the cloth napkins I had stuffed into my pocket while getting drinks for the ladies and gave it to her to wipe her tears and blow her nose.

"Thank you, Joey."

Suddenly, sunlight began streaking through the clouds again, falling like a gentle waterfall over us. I took her in my arms and held her tight. I could feel her arms slowly coming up my back to hug me as well.

"Let's take a walk around the block," I said. And holding hands, we walked and walked in silence. Finally, I asked her, "Did you tell anyone about the abortion?"

"After I went to confession, I told my mother," she said, sounding tired and somewhat matter-of-fact. "She was very upset. I told her I was very selfish. I could've had the baby and put it up for adoption, but that meant the band wouldn't be able to rehearse and perform. And my sisters and I worked years for this. I will have to live with myself knowing I killed a child. I hate myself for it. I still cry at night."

"When you called me last Saturday night, and I was making suggestions to help you sleep, I said think about dreams that made you happy. But you were quiet, and…it sounded like you were crying. Were you?"

"Yes. Thinking what my child's happy moments would have been and her dreams," she said, wiping her tears away. "But I will never be that selfish and destroy a life again. When I told my sisters later, I felt so ashamed. I said, 'Make sure the guy you love respects your values. And don't dare change who you are for him. Because then you're surrendering to being controlled by him, so you don't lose him. And that's when you self-destruct.' I'm sorry, Joey.

I wanted to come over and be happy with you, and I'm ruining your Thanksgiving."

"I'm glad you came over. I haven't had too much confidence in myself since I came to live with my grandmother. And I was taking it out on you and your sisters to work super hard during rehearsals. I was also preparing myself today to hear your 'not good news' that you were dating Mark, were having problems with him, but were going to stay with him, and were waiting until now to tell me that you couldn't see me, but wanted to keep me and my music in the band. Or something like that."

"Joey, I'd never do that to you!" Her tender smile embraced me as her hand gently came up to brush an oncoming tear away from my cheek. "I'm no fool. You're the first honest, decent guy I've ever enjoyed being with."

With joy's serious gaze, I took her hand, and said, "I have to tell you something. It came with a price." We started walking through the neighborhood as I began talking about my abandonment of values and self in Chicago while my band was self-destructing. With difficulty, I shared my experimenting with drugs and my alcohol abuse, that grew more serious when Kay left. Then my nightmare and the epiphany on the bus ride to Baltimore late in the a.m. hours of the night. The bus would be riding through neighborhoods or passing them in the nearby distance, and I'd be staring out the window at them while my reflection would be staring in at me. As we passed through neighborhoods in a town, I'd stare through my reflection into the windows of lighted rooms in homes and imagining the families and children in them. Especially the children. Children like me wanting to grow up pursuing a dream. Work hard on something they loved so they could share it with others. Have them admire it. Appreciate it. And get paid for it.

"Then my reflection started screaming at me. 'Look at what you're doing to me! You're killing me! You hear me?! You're killing me!' I became so frightened I grabbed my duffel bag, opened it, and took out all the containers of prescription meds for depression, LSD pills, and others to get me high and down, opened the window, and threw them out. After a couple of hours, I started shaking with chills and became sick. I was moaning with painful withdrawal symptoms, and I quickly opened the window to puke my guts out. When the bus finally pulled into the Greyhound Bus Terminal in Baltimore, I went into the men's room, fell to the floor in a stall, curled myself around a toilet, and again began heaving and retching my insides out. Then, when I realized I couldn't get any lower to the ground unless I died, I slowly struggled to get up and hobbled out to the sidewalk. I turned and just walked until I reached an intersection, where I hailed a cab to Grandma's. And here I embraced her and God to save myself while I pray and say the rosary every night," I said, noticing that we were standing a little way from a streetlamp that hadn't turned its light on yet.

We must've walked a few blocks from Grandma's house. My eyes rested on Chris, whose eyes took hold of mine. Then she embraced me, laying her head against my chest. I hugged her tight, so she'd know how I felt about her. She shortly pulled away, but she grabbed my hand, and we walked.

"When I wanted to sing and play in the folk band at church, I wanted to get as close to Christ as I could every Sunday. Father Love introduced me to a couple of women and another girl my age who had an abortion, and we talked about taking responsibility for what we did, asking for forgiveness, and living a life that is an example for others to follow. Now, I look forward to going to church, receiving communion, getting closer to Christ, and making my faith stronger in Him by helping other girls my age not make the same mistake I did."

Suddenly, I stopped walking and did something spontaneous. I gently took her face between my hands and kissed her. Then I hugged her, saying, "You're beautiful." As I was backing away, she put her arms around me, drew me close, and kissed me, slowly and tenderly, and then just laid her head on my chest.

Gray-blue twilight was surging over the horizon as we started walking back to Grandmas. I said, "We may not have time for dessert. Grandma said her friends wanted to be back home before it gets dark."

"That's okay, Joey. You'll owe me."

"Wait. Grandma said that if I asked you out, which was inviting you over here for dessert today, she would fix us dinner. So, since you work weekends, would you like to come over for dinner one night next week?"

"I would love to. Call me."

"I will." I walked her to her car and said, "Oh, how did you know I'd say, 'Good decision' when you said you were going to leave the band and go to college?"

"Because you're disciplined and practical, Joey. And you're honorable. But it's your quirky sense of humor that makes me believe there's hope."

"Hope? Hope for what?"

"Us staying together." Our eyes embraced each other with a smile as I opened the car door for her. "Oh, please say bye to your grandmother for me, and tell her I'll see her one-night next week. And say bye to her friends for me."

"I will."

I watched her drive away as a feeling of joy swelled and rolled through me. Walking toward the house, I realized that we didn't even talk about when our next rehearsal would be.

CHAPTER 21

I entered the dining room, and Grandma's friends were getting up from the table as Grandma was getting off the phone. "Oh, here you are, Joey. I just called my neighbor, Charley. Al and Spike are on their way over. Where's Chris?"

"She had to leave. But I told her you'd fix us dinner one night next week."

"Oh, that's grand, Joey. I'll look forward to that."

"Chris's a peach, Joey. A real keeper. I sense it," said Rose, smiling.

"I can always tell by the way a girl's eyes light up when they meet a guy they like," said Lorine. "And when my two nephews brought their girlfriends around for me to meet, I always told them which one I thought they'd better marry if they wanted to be happy. And they did. And they're still married! And that's why I think Chris is right for you."

I smiled and said, "Thank you, Lorine."

I got the ladies' coats, scarves, and hats and helped each one on with theirs.

"Thank you, Joey. We know it's early, but, unfortunately" — and here she paused — "and most regrettably, age with physical disabilities dictate to us now what we can and cannot do," said Jeanine slowly and rose a little unsteadily, leaning on her cane.

"What Jeanine really means is that she had one too many old fashioneds, Joey," said Rose, laughing, and the other ladies joined her.

"Well, Nina, that's a credit to you and this sumptuous feast you and Joey so kindly prepared for us," said Lorine. "Good food, good drink, and grand conversation."

Grandma beamed with pride. "Thank you, and hopefully, we can get together real soon. Maybe for lunch," Grandma said. The ladies agreed enthusiastically as the doorbell rang. "Well, here's Al and Spike."

"Wait a minute, girls!" hollered Jeanine. "Spike is mine!"

"Jeanine!" fired Rose's voice in a loud whisper. "Act your age! He's a married man."

I had to laugh. You are never too old to feel young when drinking.

"He is? I didn't know that. All right, Joey, let those handsome devils in," dictated a less fervent reaction from Jeanine.

When I returned from taking the ladies home, Grandma was humming a song to herself while washing the dishes.

"What are you humming, Grandma?"

"A song from the 1920s called 'I Love My Baby.' When Harry and I were dating, we used to love dancing in dance contests. We won our first trophy, dancing to that song. It's funny, Joey. Whenever I feel good, I always start humming or singing that song."

"Is that the silver trophy on your bureau in your bedroom?"

"Yes, it is."

"You should display that in the living room, Grandma. So your friends can see it."

"Ah, that was so long ago, Joey. Now, I just enjoy waking up and looking at it. Start my day with a good memory of Harry and me. And not dwell on my aches and pains."

I changed my shirt and pants and took over washing the dishes as Grandma dried them.

"Oh, Joey. While you and Chris were outside, the ladies and I were sharing what we were thankful for, and I meant to ask you and Chris when you came back but forgot."

Wow. I wasn't thankful for anything when I first came here. I didn't even want to be alive. But now?

I came over to Grandma and gave her a big hug and a kiss. "I'm very thankful for you, Grandma. For letting me live here, using your car, and saving my life." And I let the tears flow. I broke away from holding Grandma, got a napkin, dried my face, and blew my nose.

"Ah, Joey, that is very sweet of you, honey." She began crying, and I handed her a napkin as well. "You stay here as long as you like," she said, sobbing.

"Thank you, Grandma. And thanks for asking me to take you to church. I met Chris there, and I even started to pray and say some of the rosary listening to it on your radio at night before I went to bed. Then I read some of the prayers from the book you left on my nightstand."

"Wonderful. Oh, Joey," she said with a slight thrill of joy. "We'll have to talk about what you and Chris would like for dinner next week."

I didn't have a clue. "Grandma, why don't you surprise us? You're a great cook."

"Joey, it won't be much of a surprise since you're going to have to go to the store for me."

"Oh, that's right." I laughed. "But we'll like anything you cook, Grandma."

"I'll start thinking about it and getting a list ready for you, Joey."

I said okay, and we finished cleaning up, and Grandma went to take a shower and go to bed. I couldn't wait to surprise her next week by paying for the groceries she'd use to fix dinner for Chris and me. I was also going to help her save money for heating oil this winter so she wouldn't have to worry about freezing in this house.

After my shower, I laid on the bed, and just immersed myself in all that happened today to make it the most wonderful Thanksgiving I'd ever had. And to think that I had wanted to kill myself because the band broke up and Kay left me! I would've missed all this today. I opened the prayer book that Grandma had given me, and I said a few prayers. I noticed Grandma didn't have her radio on again, and I thought to ask her why tomorrow. Chris shoved herself into my thoughts, and I couldn't believe how incredibly lucky I was to have met her.

I started to say the rosary when I stopped.

No. I wasn't lucky at all. Thank you, Jesus, for saving my life!

THE END

Steven Prevosto is the author of the four-star reviewed novel, The Defending Guns, a Western, also published by World Castle Publishing, LLC.

"Something happens on about every page, and I became intrigued on the first page. I had a hard time putting the book down." Bertha Jackson, OnlineBookClub.org.

"A Western with plenty of action and adventure. Bodies fall from gunfire as rapidly as metal paddles downed in a cowboy shooting gallery. Although a Western novel, it also handles contemporary issues, such as grieving for a spouse, a low attitude toward women, and dislike of Indians by those living in the American West." Donna Ford, www.theUSReview.com.

Steven's Christmas story, Christmas in The City, is published in the 2021 Anthology of Christmas Stories by Texas Sisters Press. His LBGTQ short story, Something Pulled Away, was published in the January 2022 Issue of www.scarletleafreview.com. Nina's Salvation for Joey is his second published novel by World Castle Publishing, LLC.

Steven has also written contemporary as well as classical plays. He was an actor in New York City for ten years, came home to be a woodworker, then earned his master's degree in Education and is currently a Para Educator in English for a local high school. He lives in Carroll County, Maryland, with his wife. Please, share your thoughts on Nina's Salvation for Joey by visiting him online at Prevosto@Weebly.com

www.ingramcontent.com/pod-product-compliance
Lightning Source LLC
Chambersburg PA
CBHW030329180626
46810CB00003B/1279